Confessions from a Fractured Mind

J.D.MISSEN

First Edition published 2023 (previous title 'Revelations of a Fractured Mind')
Second Edition published 2024 by Carrot Press
Book cover and image design by Carrot Publishing

ISBN: 978-1-7384353-0-2 (paperback)
ISBN: 978-1-7384353-1-9 (hardcover)
ISBN: 978-1-7384353-2-6 (ebook):

FOR DANIEL AND CHLOE

PART ONE

ALEX

CHAPTER ONE

It is Halloween. The perfect day. The perfect opportunity. What better cover could I have than to mingle amongst the revelers dressed in their garish costumes, roaming the streets as dusk begins to fall and day turns into night. I wonder if they believe, as I do, that this is a day to be revered. For this is the first day of my homecoming, my coming of age. The first step on the journey towards my final destination. This is a day that will be remembered, that will be forever marked in history, not just for myself, but for all who live in this small Suffolk town.

And so, it has come to be that I am sitting within the quiet safety of my car, parked tightly against the kerb, waiting for darkness to descend. As I wait patiently, condensation from my warm breath reaches the cold glass in front of me, misting the windscreen. Mesmerised by the patch of vapour that is rapidly spreading across the glass, I watch as my view of the street through the windscreen disappears. Then, just as the final patch of clarity is obscured, I reach down and pull out a chamois leather from the inside pocket of the door. The smeared droplets are sufficiently cleared in one sweeping arc of my hand, it is an action I am loathe to perform too often as it leaves a transparent streak across the glass, but on this occasion the act is justified, for it is essential I am able to see clearly into the road ahead. With my onward vision restored, I nestle back down into the chair again, trying to ignore the brittle sensation of the ripped leather seat underneath my thin viscose trousers, which has begun to chafe at my lower left thigh.

Almost an hour passes before the sun starts to set behind the row of houses that bisects across the top of Seaton Road. I have spent this time wisely, running through my mind what will soon come to fruition. Now I must wait patiently for the ideal opportunity to present itself. I watch as the pale blue sky gracefully melts into horizontal streaks of pink and purple, then slowly fades into muted orange and yellow, before finally being swallowed up by the darkness. It is a sight I have never tired of seeing and one that reminds me of the last time I walked these streets - when I was a child, no older than many of the youths who are wandering these narrow lanes tonight.

The brown leather watch with its tarnished brass clasp, that is fastened to my left wrist, tells me that it is almost six-thirty. Darkness has by now completely fallen and the only light comes from the streetlamp above me and from the glow of lights behind curtains pulled across the windows of the houses that line the road.

Suddenly, I catch sight in the rear-view mirror of what I have been waiting for; a group of teenagers knocking door-to-door, throwing eggs and flour at any doors whose occupants do not respond quickly enough. I watch as a man opens his front door only to be showered in flour from head to foot, transforming him into a shocked ghost, mouth wide open in astonishment. The youths retreat up the path, doubled over with laughter as the man stands motionless in the doorway, stunned by the unexpected assault. Fleetingly I wonder how the teenagers would feel if they knew I was here. Waiting. Watching them. Would they still be so bold and fearless then?

My mouth is dry. I reach down into the blue holdall that I tucked into the footwell of the passenger seat earlier. With one hand, I unzip the central compartment, reach into the dark void and rummage about until my fingers make contact with the object I have been searching for. I pull out a flask, unscrew the cap and pour into it just enough of the tepid dark brown liquid to quench my thirst. As I place the flask back into the bag again, I glance into the wing mirror to check on the progress of the group of revelers, who are still moving towards the area where my car is parked. It is almost time.

My heart races in anticipation of what lies ahead - a pleasurable mixture of excitement and fear. Soon I will learn if all of my planning has been thorough enough. If it has not, then the consequences will be dire. I mentally check through the items that are already waiting in the boot of the car; rope for binding wrists and ankles; masking tape for the mouth; a thick bath towel covering the bottom of the boot to protect the carpet from spillages. Nothing has been forgotten, it is all there, just as I have planned.

The group are almost upon me now. I pull the mask on over my face and wait until they have moved past my car, then cautiously open the door. They do not notice the sharp click of a car door closing above the raucous howls of laughter that herald a confidence at such childish pranks that only the young can afford.

Their gaiety though is much welcomed, as it will distract from my presence. Hidden in plain sight for none to see, I will slip unnoticed through their world, as silent as a ghost. Their ghoulish laughter will no doubt also be fortuitous in masking any sounds that I do not wish to be heard.

Swiftly, silently, I join the back of the group, unnoticed. It is fortunate that I am of a slight build, no taller than the average teenager. I fit in seamlessly with my red devil mask and long black cloak that almost touches the ground beneath my feet. The trident I purchased from a small shop on the high street yesterday not only serves to enhance the outfit, but also deftly conceals a stubby hunting knife within its long, grey plastic shaft. Subconsciously I run my hand over the staff, checking that the knife is still securely held in place, but also in a position where it can be easily removed if I need it.

My step quickens as I realise the direction the group are heading in. They are making their way towards Cage Lane - to the streets of my youth, where my days were spent roaming the back alleyways, trying to escape from the hell that resided within my home. The days when I learnt to be strong. The days when the purpose of my life started to observe clarity. The days when I realised that my destiny would take a different path to the ones of my neighbours and school friends.

I remain at the rear of the group as they continue to travel along the path, passing by a small opening that it is almost hidden from view by an enormous buddleia, whose drooping flowers have begun to fade from a vivid purple to a dull grey. As the revellers move past the gap, I come to an abrupt halt, allowing the teenagers to move further away from me. They do not notice that I am no longer behind them, for I am a ghost. I was never there.

It is still there, lurking in the dark like an unwanted appendage - the narrow alleyway that is sandwiched between Cage Lane and Seaton Road. It has not changed. It is still as dark and dank as I recall. The impenetrable stench of damp, rotting wood and stale urine lingers in the air like a fog. Weeds still grow around the edges of the cracked concrete path and dark green moss still creeps up the red brick wall. It is just as I remember. The streetlights at either end of the narrow space still cast the same eerie light, conical beams reaching out hopelessly into the thick darkness as a weak beacon of hope. The light cannot penetrate through the gloom sufficiently to allow the two beams to meet in the middle of the path and it is here, where the shadows are as black as coal, that I will wait.

I strike out a hand to one side, allowing it to flail about aimlessly until my fingertips scrape onto a cold hard surface just below my shoulder-line. The soft moss is caught underneath my freshly cut nails, but I resist the urge to free it. There is no time to stop. I place the palm of my right hand flat against the wall, observing the clammy moss intermingled into the brittle fabric of the wall that encompasses both sides of the path. Just as it's always been. Confident now of my position, I creep onwards and using the wall as a guide, I move further into the darkness. As I reach the centre of the black void, I stop and slink back into the shadows, the bottom of my shoulder blades pressing up against the cold, brick wall that separates the passageway from the back yard of the neighbouring property. My heartbeat quickens as I allow myself a delicious moment to anticipate the task ahead. There is a stirring down below, an excitement rising with expectancy at the pleasures that I know are awaiting me.

The deep, throaty sound of dogs barking in a nearby yard, penetrates through the blackness and jolts me from my thoughts. Somewhere in the distance, there is a faint wailing screech from the resident tom cats who are fighting over their territory. Nothing has changed. My breathing slows a little and I feel my shoulders relax with the comforting familiarity of the sounds that have always prevailed this neighbourhood.

Despite the sharp chill in the air, a line of perspiration forms across my brow, the warmth of the liquid instantly cooling as the microscopic droplets reach the chill air. It is only now that I notice I am clenching onto the staff so tightly, that the white of my knuckles can be seen, even in this, the dimmest of light. I loosen my grip a little and watch the ghost-like image fade away again into the darkness, then close my eyes to concentrate on slowing my heart rate. As my pulse settles back down into a resting rhythm again, I re-open my eyes and allow them to adjust once more to the darkness that surrounds me.

From my position on the path, I catch sight of a small group of children who are laughing at something, though I am too far away to hear what it is that is creating such joviality. One of them, who is dressed as a ghost, breaks away from the group and strides up to the next house. He presses down on the latch then brusquely pushes open the cast-iron gate, that has dropped on its hinges and scrapes noisily onto the concrete path below. The rest of the group hurry to catch up, then slow to a walking pace as they reach the path that is flagged either side by carved pumpkins. The flames from the candles inside the pumpkins flicker in the breeze, their shadows dancing across the white upright stone pillars of the porch door. The group linger slightly behind the boy as he raps loudly onto the stranger's wooden door and waits impatiently for it to be opened.

Briefly my attention is drawn away from the children to the adjoining property, where an infant has been awakened by the noise outside. Its' tired cry is soon accompanied by a male voice that is shouting from somewhere else within the house for the child to quiet down again. A light comes on in an upstairs room, then a shadow moves swiftly across the room to pick up the infant, who is now sobbing more quietly. The child is quickly soothed back to sleep by gentle singing, an action practiced so often by its mother that it has become an automated response.

The bedroom light switches off again and my focus is taken to the house where the children are still waiting. In the dark, I can see the bottom corner of the living room curtain twitch, then a hunched shadow shuffles forward to peer around the drapes to stare out into the gloom, trying to identify the cause of the terrifying insidious laughter that is less than two feet away. The residents inside the house are either too frightened or disinterested to make the effort to open the heavy, stained-glass door and the figure retreats into the darkness again.

Having received no response to their repeated rapping on the door, the children backtrack up the path, leaving the metal gate open. They spill out onto the road, then begin to move further away from me, their excited babble in high-pitched voices, becomes softer and softer until I can barely hear them.

My focus returns to the shallow place that has become my temporary accommodation. A damp mist is starting to curl its way through the brick-lined corridor that separates the two roads, where each street and the lives contained within it, are a world away from each other. At one end of the passageway is Seaton Road, where the residents keep their front gardens neat, with uniform lawns and pristine flower borders, their beloved second-hand cars parked proudly on their block-paved driveways for all the neighbours to see, are lovingly washed and polished every Sunday. I can almost visualise the well-kept husband in his neatly pressed clothes showing his two children, who are diligently holding a sponge and bucket, how to carefully wash and wax the car that cost their father the best part of six months' wages. Inside, their mother looks after the baby as she roasts a topside of beef that will form the basis of their meals for the next three days.

At the other end of the alleyway is Cage Lane, with its over-grown, unkept concrete backyards, strewn with urine and excrement from the dogs who are still snarling at each other, noses poking underneath the warped fence that separates them, thick chains around their necks prevent their jaws from meeting through the hole in the fence. The children in Cage Lane will not be having roast beef on Sundays, they will be lucky to have any food that has more than a morsel of nutrition in it, as their fathers idle away their earnings down the pub and their mothers sit in the kitchen drinking gin to numb themselves from the bitter world they have found themselves in.

I stand in the middle of the alleyway, stuck between these two worlds; the gentle bedtime stories and kisses goodnight in one road; the sound of raised voices and children cowering in their rooms with their hands over their ears in the other. This is the part of town where I grew up. Where my childhood ended. The house I lived in is like those on Cage Lane. I push the thought to one side. It is of no importance now. What is done is done. I need to focus on the task ahead.

It is then that it happened. Just like that. A split second later and I would have missed her. At first, I am uncertain that she is even real; a ghostly figure almost entirely enveloped by the mist and darkness, standing at the end of the alleyway, having become separated from her friends. This has to be fate. Her being there at the exact same time as me, standing in the same place as me. It is as if she is waiting for me. My heart thumps so loudly that I am fearful she might somehow hear it as I creep up beside her, my back scraping against the wall as I keep close to it to stay within the darkest part of the path. Gently I place my hand, which is now encased in a thick leather glove, around her soft plump mouth. In the light of the streetlamp, I see her eyes grow wider, pupils dilating as they adjust to the dimness of the alleyway, the white sclera flashing up against the darkness. I press my fingers more tightly into her flesh squeezing her mouth tightly shut, as a muted cry emits from underneath my fingers. I feel the warmth of her urine as it soaks into my trousers, feel her struggle into my arms as they envelop her, just as the mist had done so only a few moments before. It has taken seconds, that is all. Seconds for her life to alter forever.

It is a pity I have to resort to hitting her on the head with the butt of my knife, but she will not stop struggling and we need to move quickly. Her group of friends are beginning to realise she is missing. From the other side of the fog, I hear them calling 'Annalise', the name echoing through the foggy street. Annalise. So that is her name.

The girl is limp as I drag her back down the alley towards Seaton Road. I am conscious of the loud scraping noise from her heels dragging against the concrete path, the sound reverberating in the darkness, but I cannot stop now, I must carry on with my work. Quickly I pull her towards the line of parked vehicles and seconds later I am standing at the rear of my car, which remains unnoticed amongst the multitude of other working-class modes of transport that herald the livelihoods of those who live in this part of the town.

Unceremoniously I drop the girl onto the road at my feet, where she is hidden in the shadows away from the light of the nearby streetlamp. I fumble into my trouser pocket to locate the keys. My hand shakes as I quickly find the right key and plunge it into the lock, twisting it with such force that it is a miracle it does not break. In seconds, the boot is hastily flung open, awaiting its precious cargo. A furtive glance around reveals there are no other people close by.

I heave the girl up to the lip and shove her over the edge, allowing gravity to take her deep inside. The boot lid closes with a quiet but audible click then I hurry to the driver's side to open the door before anyone notices me. As I shut the car door, I hear voices in the distance calling for Annalise. They are getting closer. We must leave.

CHAPTER TWO

It is unseasonably warm for early October, though the temperature is doing little to thaw the atmosphere in the house where I am sitting, in the front living room. I am staring at the wall opposite the sofa that displays two generations of family photos, in the same turgid silence that first enveloped the house the week before Christmas, when the oncologist had gently explained to my mother that the cancer she had fought against for the past eighteen months, was now incurable.

"I'm so sorry, the cancer is very aggressive. We've been taken by surprise at how quickly the disease has spread.'

Mother had sat in a blue plastic hospital chair, her small, anemic hands clutching onto the wooden arms, steeling herself against the bitter blow she knew was about to come.

'We can of course offer you chemotherapy to slow down its progress, but it will have very severe side effects and in your current condition these would be difficult for you to tolerate.'

Mother sat stony faced, unmoving except for her eyes, which were staring at a calendar on the wall behind the doctor. I was not even certain that she was listening.

'I'm very sorry that it's not better news.'

'I don't want the chemotherapy,' she said, unexpectedly emerging from her stupor. Her eyes flicked towards the slight figure, who was sitting importantly behind a large teak desk. 'So, it seems that I will be joining my husband sooner than I had wished.'

The fragile woman drew in a deep breath then released it again with a loud sigh, as if she felt only disappointment at the sorry news and not the crippling fear that I knew she was hiding inside. She turned her head to stare at me for a moment, then collected her raincoat from the chair that had been squeezed into the back of the cramped room, where she had deposited it less than ten minutes prior to her life being turned upside down. 'Come on Beth, let's go home.'

A sharp rap on the door jolts me from my thoughts and for a moment I am disorientated by the sudden transition back to the present. Automatically I look towards the wingback chair next to the fireplace, but it is of course empty.

There it is again. The knocking is more persistent now, whoever is outside my front door seems to be determined to glean my attention. Slowly I rise from the sofa, trying to ignore the pins and needles in my lower legs that have become numb from sitting curled up for so long. I pad down the gloomy hallway that matches my somber mood perfectly and reach out towards the door latch, just as the knocking sound comes once again.

Opening the thick external door reveals to me a stranger, whose right fist is drawn back in readiness to knock once again. He is wearing a tan coloured raincoat, a chunky black briefcase waiting expectantly at his feet.

'Hello, sorry to disturb you, I'm just in the area today and looking to give someone a really good deal on replacing their windows.'

'Right, well as you can see,' I say, pointing towards the PVC bay window, 'We only recently had them replaced.'

'If you don't mind me saying, they haven't done too good a job of it.'

'Oh, why do you say that?'

'Well, you see that gap underneath the windowsill, that shouldn't be like that, it should sit flush to the wall. If you've got a moment, I could come in and show you the samples I've got,' he says, picking up the briefcase and holding it up to my eye-line.

The dark clouds that have been passing over the house whilst we are talking, decide at that precise moment to unleash their heavy burden. I could not decide whether to feel sorry for the man standing there in the rain, his navy-blue pin-striped suit with its sharp creases ingrained in all the right places, getting wetter and wetter, or to laugh at the spectacle. Either way, I felt obliged to offer him shelter from the torrent.

'You'd better come in,' I say, smiling for the first time in months. 'Do you want to take your coat off and hang it up by the door?'

'Thank you,' he says as he takes a long stride across the threshold into the hallway. Droplets of water drip off his short, dark hair and land onto the floor below. It reminds me of how a dog will shake itself when it gets wet.

'The sitting room is in there.' I point towards the first door in the hallway.

'That's very kind of you.' The salesman looks up at me, his dark brown eyes twinkling, a broad grin spreading across his flushed face.

He follows me down the corridor and into the sitting room, where I flick on the ceiling light to lift the gloom a little. 'Please make yourself at home while I make us a pot of tea.'

I watch as he settles himself into the wingback armchair that was once my mother's, then retrace my steps back out into the hallway with a much lighter step, my spirits lifted by the prospect of having some company for a while. My mood is almost jovial in comparison to the previous ten months - since that last Christmas when mother and I had valiantly got through the festivities as if nothing had happened, both pretending that this would not be the last one we would share, both ignoring the inevitable scenario that would unfold less than three months later.

As I pass by the small, square shaped dining room at the back of the house, I cannot help but glance at the dining table where we ate our last Christmas lunch. I can still visualise the cut-glass flutes filled with sparkling white wine and an enormous golden turkey that could have fed six people for a week. There were white tureens of over-boiled sprouts and carrots, a boat of thick, brown gravy and a delicate dish for the cranberry jelly, which sat as always in the middle of the table. Mother always laid out a setting at the table for my father, as had been the custom since his passing. And as always, before the banquet could be consumed, mother had pushed back the mahogany dining chair to stand at the head of the table and asked for silence so that she could make a toast to remember those who were no longer with us.

The rear of the house is even darker than the hallway, especially with the menacing clouds still overhead and rain pelting down onto the window that overlooks the garden. As I fill the kettle, my hand shakes slightly, for I have become so used to my own solitude, that it feels almost uncomfortable to have another human in the house. My fingers are still trembling as I open the tea canister that sits in its usual place on the worktop. I extract two tea bags from it and drop them into the floral china pot that I have already warmed, using the newly boiled water from the kettle. The matching teacups are always kept in the cupboard above the table, where mother kept her best crockery that was only to be laid out for the most esteemed of guests. The last time these cups were used was when the vicar came to pay his respects, three weeks after my mother's funeral. The tardy act only served to show the modest reverence he held for my mother, but still, I had dutifully rolled out the finest crockery and a selection of biscuits that mother always insisted we kept in the house, in case of any unexpected visitors.

Many packets of biscuits were consumed during the weeks before mother died. With Christmas and New Year over, mother had declined quite suddenly. I had played the part of the dutiful daughter to perfection, accompanying her to hospital appointments, organising aids to help her move more easily around the house as she became weaker, and in the latter weeks, collected prescriptions of morphine in ever increasing dosages from the pharmacy in the high street. The last few weeks seemed to last for an eternity, with a slow decline, first into a wheelchair and then a commode. Mother refused to contemplate anyone other than myself looking after her and the last few weeks were a blur of exhaustion, fear and loneliness.

Now I can barely remember how it feels not to be alone. Perhaps it is not the stranger that I had pitied, standing there on the doorstep in the torrential rain, but myself. In the few short months since mother died, the house we had once shared has become both a shrine and a prison; a memory of what once was and a reminder of what could never be again. Perhaps fate has intervened to bring this unexpected visitor to my front door.

I make my way back to the sitting room, carefully holding the worn teak tray that is now laden with a heavy teapot, matching cups and saucers, along with a plate of the biscuits. The black briefcase perched on the floor next to the front door mat, does not seem out of place though it is curious to see the long grey overcoat hanging on the mahogany coat stand, with my father's long black umbrella resting next to it, as if it had always been there.

Softly I walk back into the sitting room and place the tray onto the coffee table, then pour tea into each of the delicate cups in turn. Sitting opposite mother's wing-backed chair, perpendicular to the fireplace, I listen politely to the salesman's patter. I am not listening to the words that are being said, but instead, savouring the novelty of no longer being alone.

My eyes drift to the television in the corner of the room, where it sits on top of the mahogany stand that matches the bookcase. Always, I am reminded of how hard my mother fought to get the house she had always desired, though it had been my father's ambitions that had afforded her a lifestyle of which she felt proud. Of course, no amount of money or fine furniture could have prevented my mother's death, which could not have been described as one of peace and closure, but instead she had writhed in agony for three days, comatose, barely alive but not quite dead. In the end a doctor was called for to increase the dosage of morphine that was dripping through her veins to gently help her on her way. I recall little of what had occurred afterwards, heard nothing of the empty murmurings of sympathy from the nurses on the ward who had seen so much death already that they barely registered yet another passing. I felt numb when they handed me my mother's few possessions; her red-rimmed glasses, the 18-carat gold wedding ring my father had given her and the honey-blond wig she wore in her final few months to hide her thinning hair. That was all that was left of my mother.

The salesman is staring at me, as if aware that I am not listening, that I have drifted off to another realm just as I had done during those first few days after my mother's death, when I could not tell where one day started and another ended. The numbness that had begun to seep in during my mother's final days, had spread slowly throughout my tired body, worn down by the final weeks of caring for someone terminally ill, had become resolute, clinging onto every cell in my body. Unexpectedly, it was the task of handing back the items borrowed to ease my mother's suffering, which broke through the numbness; the guards that prevented her from falling out of the bed after I had moved her into the front living room; the commode she had used with as much dignity as she could muster and the wheelchair she refused to use, instead choosing to stay hidden away in the house to avoid the sympathetic looks from the neighbours who had guessed that she was dying. In its place, my body was wracked with an interminable grief that appeared it would never end, accompanied by infinite tears that would seemingly never cease. These were of course all to be expected, but what was not, was the rage I felt within me that I had once again been left alone.

Suddenly I realise that the man has stopped talking and is now standing in the centre of the room, looking at me expectantly for a response, but of course I have not been listening and do not know what he has said. I smile at him, hoping that he has sufficient manners to know that he needs to repeat his words.

'Well thank you for your time, I'm sure you have lots to do. Would you like me to order any windows for you?'

'Thank you but I don't need any windows, though the back door in the kitchen needs to be replaced.'

'Let's go and look at it then and I can order you another one if you like?'

'That would be great, thank you.' I lead him into the kitchen so that he can inspect the aging PVC door. I watch as he takes a tape measure out from the inside pocket of his suit jacket and jots down the dimensions of the door.

With the task complete, the man walks across the room and into the hallway, where he collects his briefcase and overcoat that is still damp despite the warmth from a nearby radiator.

'Thanks again, I'll be in touch when the door's ready to fit,' he says, opening the latch on the front door. He walks over the threshold and turns around to smile at me again, then strides off back out into the rain before I even realise that I have not asked him his name.

CHAPTER THREE

I am alone, perched on the edge of the bottom step of the staircase that sweeps up the wall that separates my house from the adjoining one. The hardness of the bowed step beneath the worn carpet is almost unbearable for the soft skin of my thighs, that are barely covered by my light-weight dress. My sharp elbows rest prone upon the top of my knees, fingers interlaced in front of my thin body. Wistfully I caress the cotton material of the white dress that is peppered with red flowers and has a matching white belt fastened securely around my slim waist. I pull the thin red cardigan around my chest a little more tightly and fasten the bottom button, which as always, has come undone.

There is no movement in the house other than from my legs, which are rhythmically jiggling up and down, trying to bring some warmth back to my bare feet, which are resting on the cold, tiled hallway floor. Automatically I cup my hands together and bring them up to my mouth. Blowing warm air into them brings a moments relief from the chill. Rubbing the back of my hands, I encourage the blood to circulate around the appendages again, but my fingertips are still tinged blue from the cold. The house is always freezing, regardless of the temperature outside. In the warmer months this can be a blessing, but for the remainder of the year, it only serves to remind me of the lonely atmosphere that has lingered over the building since my mother died.

As I gaze at the front door, an image comes to mind of me as a child, watching my mother through the partially open door. She is kneeling on the soil in front of the bay window, pushing daffodil and crocus bulbs into the warm earth, setting them amongst the snowdrops and bluebells she already planted. It was always such a glorious sight during those dark February days, to see the first pale purple crocuses pushing their way up through the previous year's decaying detritus. Later in March, they would be joined by clusters of snowdrops and daffodils and then in May, the bluebells would appear. The bluebells were always my favourite - they served as a reminder of carefree days spent playing in nearby woods that have long since been bulldozed to the ground to make room for another housing estate.

The sharp cold from the tiled floor penetrates through my now motionless feet, bringing my awareness back to the room. It often seems these days that my mind has drifted off elsewhere, as if it too cannot bear to be a part of my miserable life anymore. Where it drifts off to though I cannot say and were it not for the clock in the front sitting room, I would never have known that time passes during those moments.

I focus my mind more acutely now, noting the comforting regularity of the rhythm of my heart inside the cage that protects it. The movement reminds me of the security I once felt, wrapped up in my mother's arms after I had fallen over the handlebars of my small red bike. It has been such a long time since I have felt that way, I can barely remember what it feels like to be shown such kindness. I no longer understand the meaning of love, perhaps I have never even felt it. I do know though that there is a gaping void in my soul that desperately wishes to be filled, and that at this moment in time, I would accept any meagre offering of affection, even if it is only an illusion that will fade away again as quickly as it appears.

The house is still. An anticipatory quiet that is disturbed only by the rhythmic ticking of the gold-plated carriage clock sitting in the middle of the mantle-piece above the open fireplace - a treasured family heirloom, handed down through generations, a reminder of those that have passed and the lives they once lived. How I hate that clock and all that it represents and yet I feel unable to move it from the place where it has sat for as long as I can remember.

My ears strain to filter out the familiar sounds of the house; the rhythmic clicking of the boiler timer as it kick-starts the central heating into life; the side gate rattling as the wind rushes up the path and into the garden beyond. My mind is playing tricks on me. I cannot decide if I can hear a car approaching, or if I am merely anticipating the sound. My eyes narrow slightly, the muscles in the corners of my jaw tightening as I listen more intensely, trying to determine if the sound is real or imaginary. A car passes by the front door, a flash of red moving across the stained-glass window. In an instant it is gone. I can breathe again.

Merlin, my beloved Burmese, who I adopted as a kitten, softly pads down the stairs behind me. 'Hello Merlin, are you hungry?' I say as I gently stroke the top of his head.

Merlin pauses his journey momentarily to rub against my thigh, a deep, throaty purr emerging from within his belly. Then with his need for affection satiated, the cat continues to pad softly down the stairs and across the floor towards the kitchen, where his newly scrubbed bowl has already been re-filled with fresh meat.

As Merlin pushes open the door to the kitchen, I can hear the oven whirring as it slowly cooks the pork and apple casserole I prepared earlier. I know by now that it is one of Alex's favourites, though I will of course need to be reminded once more that the meal is not quite as good as mother's would have been.

As I sit on the stairs, my mind flits back and forth, checking that I have done everything I should have done; all the floors and surfaces have been cleaned; the ornaments on the mantlepiece have been dusted and put back in their correct place. My stomach churns, acid bubbling up into the back of my throat as I wait for the sound of a key twisting in an old yale lock, the moment when I realise it is now too late to change anything. I pray that tonight Alex might be in a more pleasant mood than I have seen of late, though my instinct tells me that I will be disappointed.

The ever-present ticking of the clock in the sitting room interrupts my thoughts. I peer around the newel post to stare at it from my position on the bottom step. It feels as if the clock is watching me, yet its presence also draws me to it. I can feel its gaze upon me, penetrating into my thoughts, reminding me that I am not allowed to think or to feel. Reminding me that I am a ghost. For this is what I have become; a soulless shell, with nothing inside. I am no longer living, I merely exist.

The clock emits a soft chime as the second-hand heralds a new hour. Alex is late, a frequent occurrence these days, always with a plausible excuse if I dare to question it. I can no longer tell if Alex is lying. Perhaps I no longer care.

Merlin has finished eating. He trots across the

hallway and rubs up against my legs as he pushes past me as he climbs the stairs. Cats are clever. They have a natural instinct that protects them from harm. Perhaps I should have listened to my instincts with Alex. I should have noticed how Merlin cowered away and hid each time Alex appeared. Merlin is right again, of course. Now I too can hear the low throbbing sound of a car pulling up outside the house.

The deep throaty diesel engine reminds me of the time that inevitably came when I could no longer nurse mother and an ambulance was summoned to take her to the hospital on the other side of the town. It was a small cottage hospital that was mainly used for outpatient appointments, recuperation and respite care. And of course for those who would never again leave the building through the ornate archway that arcs over the front entrance like a pallid rainbow, devoid of colour or hope.

The nurse who had led us into the women's ward at the rear of the building, was jovial to the point of irritation. Did she not know that my mother was dying? Could we not just be left to get through this process with as much dignity as possible? No, it would seem that we could not, as we were led to a bed in the centre of the ward with only a thin blue curtain for privacy.

'Here we are my lovelies, you'll like this ward, it gets the sun in the morning and there's plenty of other patients to chat to.'

How I held myself back from making a cutting remark I do not know as I wheeled my mother into the ward and towards the bed where we all knew she would soon pass from this world to the next. Mother did not say a word as she weakly moved from the wheelchair to the bed. I helped her to lie down, then dutifully kissed the soft skin on her forehead, that was shrunken and pale.

'I'll be back later mother, I'll just pop home and get your toothbrush and a few other bits and pieces,' I said, knowing that this could be the last time that I could speak to her.

She did not reply, but sat staring at the wall behind me, as if there were something there. I met her gaze and for a brief moment the cloud lifted and she recognised me. Then, just as quickly, it faded again, replaced by the dull glaze I had become accustomed to over the past week. As I left her bedside, I glanced back to see the person she had become, a crumpled, shriveled shell of the elegant woman she once was. It was then that I asked the god that I had never believed in, to take this woman quickly, so that she did not have to suffer any longer and I would not have to watch her become someone that I no longer recognise. I close my eyes, allowing the memories to wash over me, then as the recollections began to fade away, I open them again.

I look around the small kitchen in which I am now sitting, the sound of the car engine prompting me to move from my perch on the staircase. Suddenly I am aware of the presence of a cup of tea on the table in front of me that I do not recall making. Picking up the vessel I optimistically take a sip, but it is of course now cold. I replace the dainty, china cup onto the glass placemat, the one with the pink and white daisies my mother had liked so much when she had seen them in a teashop in town, that she had felt compelled to use the money that had been put aside to pay the milkman. Of course, the debt was later chased up and father believed mothers lie that it was the shop who was at fault for making a mistake in their books. The debt was cleared for the sake of retaining a good relationship with a long-standing customer and my father never knew the truth of the matter.

My attention is drawn to the latte-coloured clock that is hanging on the wall above the partially glazed door that leads into the hallway. The ticking of the clock seems to grow louder with the realisation that time is running out. There is not enough time now to make another cup of tea. There is so much work to do before Alex comes back, demanding to know if I have managed to finish all the tasks that have been left for me; the hateful, never-ending list that seems to grow longer each day and keeps me tethered to a house that has long since become my prison.

Wearily, I push back the chair, wincing at the loudness of the wooden legs as they scrape across the vinyl floor. I glance again at the clock on the wall, half hoping that my first reading of it was wrong and that somehow, I have more time than I first feared. But of course, it is not wrong and I need to hurry if I am to finish all the jobs I need to do.

First, I need to prepare the vegetables to accompany the casserole that is already simmering in the bottom of the oven. I pull out the vegetable drawer and extract two large carrots and a sprig of broccoli that has begun to soften but will be fine once cooked. Quickly I peel and slice the carrots, place them into a pan of cold water then move them onto the gas hob ready for when they need to be cooked. The broccoli I will add later once the carrots are part boiled. I know that putting the two different types of vegetables in the same saucepan could result in another black mark against me, but equally putting them in separate pans could be deemed a waste of water and yield the same result.

I drop the vegetable peeler into the sink and stride across the room to the door that leads to the rear lobby. Within the small area is a cloakroom that was once an outside toilet, and a large walk-in cupboard that was once a larder. Pulling open the heavy wooden door, I reach inside for the light pull and immediately the dark cavern is bathed in light. At the back of the larder is a mop and bucket, which I pull out and carry back into the kitchen. Swiftly I fill the bucket with warm water, adding just enough cleaning fluid to clean the floor adequately without making it sticky, which would of course elicit another bad mark against me.

Placing the bucket onto the floor, I pick up the mop and plunge it into the water, squeeze out the excess water, then sweep it across the floor in an arc shape. The floor is only half clean when I hear a car door slam shut in the distance, followed by footsteps clipping up the path. Too late. I have allowed time to run away from me.

'I cannot believe what I am seeing,' Alex says slowly in disbelief. 'You've had the entire day to clean the house. That's all you had to do and you couldn't even do that properly.'

I know that I have failed. Alex reminds me so frequently of my failures that I no longer need for them to be verbalised, they are so deeply ingrained in my psyche.

Footsteps move up the stairs, two steps at a time. Seconds later a bathroom door slams shut, rattling in its doorframe from the force of the movement. The sound makes me flinch and I drop the mop to the floor, where it clatters onto the hard surface. The sound stirs me from the stupor I have found myself to be in. Carefully I place the bucket, still filled with soapy water, onto the floor next to my feet and watch as a little of the liquid sloshes out over the lip and onto the newly cleaned floor. Tentatively I move towards the table again. My legs are in a gelatinous state and do not seem to want to move from the spot where they are rooted, but I spur them on and eventually they follow my command to carry me to the nearest chair.

I am mindful of the coldness of the varnished wooden chair that is penetrating through my thin dress as I sit motionless, listening to the sound of running water coming from above. The noise is barely audible above the sound of my heart thumping. Indecision rushes through me. I do not know what to do. I cannot decide which action would anger Alex the least at this moment in time. I cannot move, fear pinning me to my seat.

Suddenly I realise that the shower has been turned off and footsteps are striding across the landing. The familiar sound of a door being closed evokes memories of my mother and the over-sized well-polished tall boy in the front bedroom, which she had insisted on keeping after my father died as she said she could not bear to part with it. My father had won that piece of furniture in a card game and mother never forgave him for bringing it home as it was a reminder of his previous game, where he had lost a week's wages and the ancient car that would transport us on day trips and holidays at the seaside, neither or which happened again after that night. Mother detested that heavy-set piece of furniture as much as I do now. But still she kept it as it had reminded her of my father. Now it only serves to remind me of Alex.

I hold my breath as I hear footsteps trip down the stairs. For a split second there is silence, then comes the sound of a front door being slammed shut once again. I cannot move, frozen to the chair, not knowing what to do next. There is an immediate sense of relief that Alex has gone, coupled with fear that I have been deserted once again. I am overwhelmed with the feeling of failure that I have not done what was required to make Alex happy. I am a failure. I must try better next time.

The insistent bleeping of the smoke alarm startles me. The casserole that I have spent the afternoon cooking is still in the oven. Forgotten. Like me. I retrieve the floral oven glove from the worktop, fling open the door and pull out the dish, ignoring the searing pain as the heat from the ceramic dish penetrates through the thin material of the oven glove that received on my last birthday.

Gently I place the dish onto the counter-top and lift the lid to peer inside to see if it is still edible. I know that Alex will expect a meal to be ready whenever it is desired and that it must be in a fit state to eat at whatever time that might be. Retrieving a plastic ladle from a nearby drawer, I drag it through the thick, dark liquid. There is not enough time now to make another one, I will hope that when Alex returns sufficient gin has been consumed as to not notice the slightly congealed texture of the gravy. My mother would have thinned out the gravy with the cooking water from the vegetables, but there is always a danger of diluting the taste if too much liquid is added. The choice is an impossible one as either could result in further punishment, so I decide to leave it as it is.

I dollop a large portion of the pork concoction onto a plate, along with an enormous mound of new potatoes, and vegetables, then cover it with a stoneware plate on top, just as mother would have done. Carefully I carry it across the room and place it onto the bottom shelf of the fridge, ready to be re-heated later if required. I will know in the morning if the food has been up to standard as either the dirty, empty plate will be left on the worktop for me to wash, or it will be in the bin alongside the discarded food.

A turgid silence has descended over the house. It does not feel right to interrupt it with the forced gaiety of the evening television programmes that I used to watch with mother. And in any case, I do not feel that I deserve to enjoy the comedies and soap operas that kept my mother and I entertained, as we sat side by side in silence, staring at the small box in the corner of the sitting room.

So instead, I sit in mother's wingback chair in the front living room until darkness replaces the light of day, then creep up the stairs as if afraid to awaken the ghosts within the four walls of this house. The light from the moon shining through the stained-glass window of the front door, is all the light that I need to find my way up to my bedroom. Once inside, I pad across the room and switch on the small lamp that rests on the bedside table. Suddenly I am overcome with weariness. I lie down on top of the bedspread covering the mahogany half-tester bed, still fully clothed and do not stir again until the first rays of dawn begin to emerge.

CHAPTER FOUR

She is still alive. Only just, but still, I can scarcely believe it is true. She has lasted far longer than I thought possible. I am becoming more proficient. I am learning. It is a pity that I cannot keep her, but I have more work to do. Our time together is nearly over. I almost feel a tinge of sadness at the thought that this moment cannot be retained indefinitely and that it will soon pass. I know this must be the case with the same certainty that I understand that time cannot be paused, but must be ever moving, an omnipresent reminder of the tasks that still lie ahead.

I push the thought to one side and instead allow my mind to flit to the evening I have planned for the two of us. Our last night together. My pulse races as I imagine her lying prone across the mattress, her wrists bound above her head, tied to the metal pipe that runs the entire length of the wall. Perhaps on this occasion I will allow her ankles to be left unbound. Perhaps she will even enjoy it as I gently squeeze her neck, feeling the hyoid bone crack under the firm but light pressure from my fingers.

My heart rate quickens at the thought of seeing her reaction at the moment when she realises that she is about to die. This is the ultimate moment, the one that is held in such reverence. The moment of realisation, that her journey is finite, that there is no other way for her to escape from this room except through death.

The moment when she discovers that it is I who will rescue her from the place where she has been imprisoned the past few days. It is I who will set her free; free of the bonds that hold her to a life that is no longer worth living. Just as I had once wished for that release to come to me. But it never did. This is the moment I crave and dread in equal measure of bittersweet anticipation. The instance when I see the light slowly extinguish from her eyes as I help her to move onto the next chapter of her journey. It is also the moment when I will be alone once more. Alone in this cellar that I have both feared and revered throughout my life, that I detest with all my being and yet, it is the one place where I am able to be myself. In the cellar there is no need for me to pretend to be somcone I am not, to live the same monotonous life that others seem to aspire to lead. In the cellar I can be whoever I wish to be.

A soft whimper from the other side of the room attracts my attention away from my thoughts. I glance over at the girl, as if noticing her for the first time. Her long dark brown hair is still swept up in a ponytail at the back of her head, the translucent pale blue bobble still visible amongst her locks. Her ghoulish costume is soiled and damp from the acidity in the room and the sweat from her fear. The whiteness of the unbleached cotton material looks almost ghost-like against the grimy brick wall behind her. She is sitting propped up against the wall, on the old mattress that I hauled down the steep staircase from the front bedroom. She is watching me, just as I watch her. Her brow furrows slightly, wondering what it is that I am going to do next.

Momentarily I turn my back on her and stride over to the workbench at the far end of the room. I have already prepared the instruments. They are all laid out neatly on the wooden bench my grandfather made for his own work. I pause for a moment, deciding which I should choose first. I pick up the hand-saw closest to me, its newly cleaned and oiled blade gleams in the dim-light. Running my index finger along the blade, a thin crease of red appears on the soft pad. I watch as it trickles along my finger and drops onto the cold, concrete floor below. I imagine my grandfather chastising me for making a mess on his floor and automatically rub the tip of my shoe across the stain, smearing the droplets into the dirt until it they are no longer visible.

Still holding the tool in my hands, I glance over my shoulder at the girl and see a flicker of fear flash across her face. Her breath quickens, eyes widen as she tries to guess my intentions though at the same time not wishing to know. I remember that dilemma all too well, here in this same cellar; a child's insatiable curiosity at wanting to learn everything about the world around them. But there are some things in this world that perhaps a child does not want to know about, that they should not know about. Regardless, it is time for me to give something back to this world, to teach others what I have learnt. Whether they wish to or not.

I walk towards her, savouring each step that I take, I move closer and closer until I am standing in front of her. The girl's nostrils flare, her chest heaves as she breathes faster, her mouth straining against the tape as she tries to scream, forgetting that she cannot do so. Her eyes widen as she realises that even if she could scream, no one can hear her. No one knows that she is here. Her breathing becomes more laboured, her pink cheeks reddening almost to a deep purple as she struggles to contain the fear that is tightening her airways to such an extent that her brain is now receiving insufficient oxygen to allow for more than the most basic of functions to be nurtured. Her shoulders sag as she nears the point of unconsciousness. She shrinks her rounded back into the damp roughness of the red bricks behind her, as if hoping that somehow a miracle will occur and the wall will give way, swallow her whole, envelop her into the darkness of the abyss and save her from the nightmare she has found herself in. Then she looks up at me, her eyes that were once a curious mixture of fear and steely determination, have given way to realisation and quiet acceptance; no one can save her from what is about to come.

CHAPTER FIVE

It is only when a dull thud heralds the arrival of the morning newspaper dropping onto the doormat, followed by the low squeak of the letterbox as its well-oiled spring snaps back into place, that I realise Alex has not returned. The instinctive realisation comes from the silence that prevails across the house, a lack of heavy footsteps padding across floorboards, an absence of creaking hinges that hold fast the bedroom door at the front of the house. With a sense of trepidation, tinged with anxiety that perhaps somehow, I have missed the familiar sounds, I pull back the floral bedspread that I must have climbed underneath at some point during the night, then swing my legs over the side of bed. I firmly plant both feet onto the thin rug where my slippers are, as always, neatly lined up, ready and waiting to be worn.

Even though I know that I am alone, I still sneak across the floor as if afraid of somehow awakening a ghost. I choose a pair of faded jeans from the bottom drawer of my teak chest and select an old pale blue jumper that is neatly folded on the top shelf of the wardrobe. I dress quickly, as I have been accustomed to so that I do not waste a precious moment of the day. It does not matter what I wear, I rarely leave the house anymore.

As I creep down the stairs, I am mindful of the creaky board that is second from the last step and take care to step over it. The only sound echoing through the house is the constant rhythmic ticking of the clock in the sitting room. Even Merlin has not appeared as he would normally do, curling his tail around my leg to ask for his food bowl to be replenished. It occurs to me that I have not seen Merlin since the day when I sat on the bottom step. Perhaps he has also left me and found comfort in another place.

As I reach the last step, I immediately catch sight of the newspaper that is lying on the door mat, its front page ripped almost into two by the forcefulness of being shoved through the letterbox by a paperboy who is barely fourteen and has never had a job before. I stoop down to pick it up and pad softly into the kitchen, ignoring the familiar stark coldness of the tiled floor beneath my bare feet.

It is still dark. The first rays of daylight have not yet begun to emit their warm glow across the sky, peeling back the layer of darkness that now shrouds the northern hemisphere. I push open the kitchen door and switch on the ceiling light, a comforting glow immediately fills the room. The door behind me swings shut. I turn to look at it, half expecting to see a figure standing there in the shadows of the hallway, but it is empty. Automatically I glance up at the clock above the door and note that it is 7.30 am.

A gentle creak, followed by the quiet click of a latch snapping back into place as a front door is gently closed, startles me. Stealthily I reach over and slowly switch off the light, hoping that the faint noise is inaudible. My heart thumps against my rib cage as I stand motionless behind the door, listening for footsteps. My patience is rewarded as I hear the creak of a step, followed by the soft rhythmic clump of footsteps treading up the stairs. I let out the breath that I have been holding, unaware that I have been doing so, then take a few steady breaths, allowing my pulse to settle again.

The footsteps move across the landing and a sharp click from above tells me that a door has been shut, followed by the sound of running water as a bath is being filled. In my mind's eye I see Alex undress, carefully folding each item of clothing one by one, then placing them into the wicker laundry basket on the landing, ready to be washed. The tap is turned off and I imagine a slim frame sliding into the warm water, which must of course, always be at the correct temperature. This is yet another task that I have failed to master, I can no longer be trusted to even try to rectify my past mistakes.

As I switch the kitchen ceiling light on again, I place my hand over the plastic casing to try to muffle the sharp click that I know will follow. I long to be invisible, to disappear so that I might avoid the punishment that I know will come, for whatever misdemeanor deserves it. Recently Alex's behaviour has changed and I sense that I am being discarded, which wounds me deeply. Perhaps I am to be replaced, cast off like a small box of carboard packaging that having been used, will be squashed flat and thrown away so thoughtlessly that it is barely noticed by anyone.

It is an odd thought that perhaps my life might change. My soul is a chasm of unfathomable emotions; despair that Alex's perception of me is of such disappointment that I must now be superfluous; and a sense of relief that soon I will no longer endure this soulless prison, that I may escape from this empty carcass that was once was filled with gaiety and laughter and now only hears silence. I do not even have the energy to cry anymore, even this most primitive of emotions has been beaten from me. All I hear now is the omnipresent ticking of the carriage clock in the sitting room, that echoes the beating of my heart as it thumps with the constant fear inside of me. And once they have stopped, there will only be silence. There will be no sounds to fill the void, for I will be a ghost who no longer exists. And what of Alex? I am beginning to consider that perhaps Alex never existed at all, but is only a mirage, a reflection of my own needs and desires, a mirror of my soul that was laid bare in my most vulnerable moments after my mother died and left a void that was just waiting to be filled.

There seems little point in going back to bed now so I pad across the floor and fill the kettle with cold water from the kitchen tap, then place it onto the worktop before switching it on. From an overhead cupboard I select a mug, then retrieve the milk from the fridge, defiantly pouring a little into the mug, an act that always serves to irritate Alex, whose mother held steadfast the notion that the milk should always be added last. I am not brave enough however to deviate from the remainder of the process, and having dropped the teabag into the water, I check the kitchen clock to ensure that the concoction is brewed for exactly one minute in water that has just boiled. I know from experience that Alex will be able to tell from the colour of the tea if these exact instructions have not been followed and this is not a risk I wish to take.

Somewhere overhead, an over-bath shower has been switched on, the roar of water echoing through the ceiling as it cascades into the enamel bath. I have been taught that the water must never be too hot as that would not only be an unnecessary expense, but apparently this is also not the most conducive way to wash your hair, though I have never received an explanation as to why this is the case. I have learnt over the years not to question the reasoning behind Alex's thinking. Just because something may not make sense in my mind, it may be perfectly acceptable to Alex.

Soft baritones drift downwards through the artex ceiling that has discoloured above the cooker from a soft white to a yellowy brown stain. The shower is switched off again and footsteps patter across the floorboards. I imagine Alex reaching across the room for one of the towels that are always neatly folded over the radiator to ensure it is kept warm in the colder months. I make a mental note that a fresh towel needs to be removed from the stack of freshly laundered towels in the airing cupboard. The airing cupboard is a constant source of anxiety for me, the towels must always be kept soft and fluffy and folded in the same way that Alex's mother did. The tea towels for the kitchen are located on the upper shelf and must be folded neatly into quarters, the bed linen, which must always be ironed, is always to be placed on the lower shelf.

Footsteps once again trip downstairs. There is a breath's pause and I imagine blue checked slippers kept next to the front door, at right angles to the front door mat, being put on.

It is only when the kitchen door is opening that I realise that I am holding my breath again. My hands are shaking so much that I place down the mug of half-drunk tea, so that the contents do not spill across the clean surface of the table at which I am now sitting. I do not know what to expect. I have come to realise that Alex's mood cannot be predicted, therefore I do not know how to behave in order to prevent whatever will transpire. I look up from the table and release the breath that I have been holding.

It is only Merlin, who has emerged from wherever he was hiding, searching for fresh food.

Hurriedly I locate a tin of food in one of the cupboards, then collect the can opener, which is always kept in the cutlery drawer. As I open the can, Merlin curls his tail around my legs, rubbing against my calves at the same time. I place the newly replenished bowl onto the floor, but it seems that it is not what Merlin wants after all. He saunters past the bowl and sits next to the door that leads to the garden.

'Ok Merlin, I'll let you out. Perhaps you will eat your food afterwards.' I turn the key in the lock, push down on the handle and pull back the door just wide enough for the cat to travel through. A strong gust of wind almost takes the door out of my hand. Quickly I push it shut and lock it again.

'Good morning my darling Beth, I'll have a pot of tea when you're making one,' Alex says cheerfully.

I try to hide my shock at Alex's sudden appearance and traverse the room again to the flick on the kettle in order to dutifully oblige.

'What are your plans for today?' Alex asks politely. It feels like a lifetime since Alex last asked what 'we' were doing at the weekend. Of late it has been made clear that I am not worthy of spending time with. Nausea churns in the pit of my stomach as I acknowledge the disappointment that I have become to Alex.

'I thought I might go to the car boot sale at Melton and buy some more plants.' My mouth feels dry as I wait for a reaction, not knowing if I have said the right thing or not. The rules change so rapidly it is difficult to keep up.

'Do we have money to waste on plants? I thought you wanted to save up for a new TV?'

Swallowing the temptation to bring forth a retort that I am not the one who wants a new TV, especially given that I barely watch the one that is already in the front sitting room, I manage to produce a weak smile to try to placate both Alex and the fear that is bubbling up inside me. I feel like a child again who has been chastised for breaking rules that I did not know existed.

The room is filled with silence. The conversation is over. In the distance, a living room door slams shut, the wooden frame rattling with the force of the action. I try to blink back the tears, but they seem to be determined to disobey me and I cannot prevent them from cascading down my cheeks in a torrent of emotion. Without thinking, I reach behind me to pick up the tea towel from the worktop and dab it onto my face, feeling the coarseness of the material against my soft cheeks. I bury my face into the towel and for a few moments I take in the faint odour of washing powder and simply enjoy the feeling of my warm breath as it hits the material.

My emotions under control once more, I push myself up from the chair and take hold of the kettle to refill it with the jug of water that is always kept in the fridge. I have learnt by now that the water must be filtered and chilled, regardless of whether or not it is then boiled in a kettle. It is one of the many things Alex has taught me and the memory of the punishment I received, the first and only time I forgot, is forever etched into my mind. I shiver involuntarily at the recollection, then quickly push the memory back into its box.

The sound of a door opening jolts me from my thoughts and my awareness centres on the kettle once again, which has now boiled. Carefully I remove the cream-coloured teapot from the glass display cabinet. It is a wonder that I do not drop the teapot as my fingers tremble so much. It is heavy in my tiny hands, but it is one that was given as a present, so I am not allowed to buy another one.

The temperature of the water in the kettle has now fallen below boiling point, so I pour it into the teapot, then drop two tea bags inside and watch as they sink into the void below. I am mesmerised by the teabags as they begin to swirl around the vessel in ever increasing circles, until they reach the outside of the pot. It is as if an undercurrent is pushing them inexplicably through the water to an unknown destination. The translucent fluid begins to darken, at first just a small trickle flows from the bottom corner of one of the bags, but the stream quickly hastens to a roar as the microscopic tea particles follow the same swirling pattern around the water towards the outer curve of the china pot. I watch until all the water has turned a golden beige, then replace the lid with a quiet clink.

'Don't forget to leave it for two minutes before stirring it.' The voice makes me jump and the teaspoon that I am holding, clatters onto the melamine worktop. I did not realise that I was no longer alone.

Measuredly, I inhale, then slowly exhale again, steadying my heart rate to a slower rhythm. I pick up the teaspoon and rinse it under the hot water tap, then dry it carefully on a tea towel. On the worktop, I open the sugar canister and measure two heaped teaspoons of demerara sugar into a cup. There is nothing more for me to do now but wait for the tea to brew. I glance behind me at the clock on the wall to check if the required two minutes have passed yet. They have and I have not noticed.

'I was wondering if you'd forgotten.' A loud sigh

cuts through the turgid atmosphere. I have lost yet another point, I wonder what punishment will be in store for me this time.

Carefully I remove the lid of the teapot, so as not to clink it against the fragile china, then stir it three times in an anti-clockwise direction, just the way Alex's mother apparently always did. As I stir the tea, I remember about the newspaper still lying on the doormat and fleetingly wonder if I might find the opportunity to read it and learn what is happening in the outside world. I vividly recall the singular time I had dared to retrieve the paper after Alex left. I had spent a pleasant half an hour flicking through the creased sheets that had revealed to me who had been elected Mayor that municipal year and how many burglaries had occurred in the town over the last three months. Somehow though Alex had found out what I had done, and I soon discovered that I had broken yet another rule that I did not know about. I could never have imagined the punishment that such a seemingly minor misdemeanor would entail and even now I shudder at the memory of it. The sensation of utter loneliness that I had felt sitting alone in the darkness has never left me. I had not even known if the sun had risen, for daylight could not penetrate through the thick oak planks that encase the void under the stairs that has been fashioned into a cupboard. At first, I had sobbed, the salt from my tears drying into pearly white crystals in the corners of my eyes, my shoulders aching from the tension held within them. After a while though my shoulders relaxed and I became quiet with acceptance, for I knew by then that there was no one to hear my cries.

'I think I will go out for a walk this afternoon. I know that you won't wish to join me.'

The voice brings me back into the kitchen again

and the vision of the cupboard under the stairs fades away. Alex is right as always. Any fleeting notion I had considered earlier about purchasing plants for the garden is long gone and the familiar apprehension that I feel at the thought of leaving the house has returned. It has now been several weeks since I have been further than the front path and I have become afraid of what lies beyond the garden gate.

Gingerly I pick up the teapot and cradle it with both hands, then carry it over to the table, ignoring the searing pain in my fingers as the scalding heat seeps through the delicate ceramic walls. Gently I position the teapot onto a placemat and place an unused teaspoon in front of it. The matching china cups are in the cupboard above the kitchen table. I squeeze past two chairs and pull out two cups and saucers. I place one cup down nearest to me, the other I set down at the far end of the table. I have already poured sufficient milk into a small bone china jug that is decorated with miniature yellow and red flowers and set it down next to the matching sugar bowl.

'I expect you've got lots of housework to finish off in any case. The bathroom looks as if it hasn't been cleaned properly for weeks.'

Instantly I recognise that particular tone in Alex's voice, the flash of irritation that dares to provoke me. I cannot respond, whatever I say will be the wrong answer. But of course, if I do not speak, then I will be accused of ignorance and will be punished for that misdemeanor instead. I decide the safest option is to force a smile upon my face in acknowledgement that I have heard what has been said. I barely recall what it feels like to not fake a smile, to laugh freely at some comedy act on the television, or to feel amusement at my cat's antics with the newly pressed washing that is neatly folded in the airing cupboard at the top of the stairs. The sensation is now so alien to me that I have begun to wonder if I will ever feel it again.

My attention is diverted from my thoughts towards the teapot, reminding me that once again I have not been paying sufficient interest to Alex's needs. The tea has not been poured and I know without the need for Alex to vocalise a chastisement, that I have been a disappointment once again.

'Right, well I'm off then,' Alex says.

I replace the teacup onto its saucer a little more forcibly than perhaps was intended and the cup rattles against the saucer to such an extent that I fear it will crack. If it did, I know I will be blamed for it and I cannot imagine the punishment for such a crime as damaging mother's best china.

'I want to see that you've smartened yourself up a bit by the time I get back, you look a right mess.'

Moments pass and suddenly I realise that I am alone, staring at the front door, as if expecting it to open. Of course, it does not and I am alone in my mother's house once more, with only the sound of the clocks rhythmic ticking filling the air.

The rest of the day passes in a blur of comforting tedium. I busy myself carrying baskets of clean washing outside to peg out on the clothesline, then bring them back in again once they have sufficiently dried in the gentle breeze, then iron them carefully, ready to put away in the airing cupboard.

I decide to run myself a bath as a treat and even manage to find some bubble bath stashed away at the back of the medicine cabinet. By the time I get out of the bath it is 4.30. Alex will return soon. I look through my wardrobe and pull out a knee-length skirt and tight-fitting top that I had almost forgotten about as it had been so long since I had been out anywhere that warranted wearing something other than jeans.

No wonder Alex thinks I have let myself go, I deduce, staring at my reflection in the mahogany full-length mirror that once belonged to my mother. My hair is in desperate need of a proper cut, but I do not know how to find either the time or money to do so. My hands are rough and dry, fingernails neatly cut short so that they do not pick up dirt underneath them when I am scrubbing the kitchen floor. I remember one Christmas that my mother had bought me a bottle of bright red nail polish and a packet of emery boards. I still recall how it felt when I had showed off my manicured hands to the other girls at school when we returned after the winter break. The most popular clique in my class, the one I could only ever dream of belonging to, had cooed over the bright colour of the polish and asked me to share it with them, and even though I knew that they were just using me and would probably never condescend to speak to me again, I gave them the little I had left. I knew that this was a rare treat never to be repeated but even so, it was worth it to me to have that one moment in time when I was popular, where I felt loved and wanted. For that brief moment, a bright shining light had been cast across my dark existence; I had been noticed by the people I held in the highest esteem, the ones I yearned to accept me into their midst. Of course, I was discarded just as quickly again once the polish had chipped so much that it had to be removed and I was left to fade away once again into the shadows, which is where I then stayed for the remainder of my school days.

The click of a front door quietly closing jolts me from my thoughts and a cold feeling of trepidation begins to spread deep inside the pit of my stomach. I do not know what to expect. The pattern of Alex's behaviour that I have so carefully studied and learnt in order to match my reactions to them to avoid further chastisement, has changed. The unpredictability of the situation leaves me with a rising sense of nausea, if I do not know how Alex is going to behave then I do not know how I can appease.

Tentatively I leave the safety of my bedroom and creep across the landing towards the stairs, curious to discover who has just come in through the front door but at the same time, afraid of what I might find. I look down the stairs to find two impeccably polished brogues resting side by side on top of the door mat. In the hallway mirror, I can see the outline of a figure.

'You think this is acceptable, do you?' Alex's sneering voice cuts through the silence.

I feel compelled to look in the hallway mirror, first downwards to the court shoes that I found earlier hidden in the back of my wardrobe, then slowly upwards to my head, where my hair is still a little damp from the bath. I cannot answer, for whatever I respond, it will be wrong.

'You can't go out looking like that! All the men will leer at you,' Alex jeers. 'Or is that what you want?'

I shake my head, my heart racing, knowing that it will not be enough to placate the mood that Alex is in.

'You look like a slut. Go and get changed now, then get me something to eat. If, of course, you're capable of doing such a simple task.'

Biting back the tears that are forming, I run upstairs without looking back and shut the bedroom door behind me. I slide down onto the carpet, arms curled protectively around my knees and sob until I can cry no more.

CHAPTER SIX

She is dying. I stand back to watch as she takes her last few breaths, a gasping rattle heralding the moment when life begins to drain out of her. I gaze intently into her eyes, observing as the cornea begins to solidify, turning from a beautiful emerald green to a pure milky white. I almost miss it, the moment that I have been waiting for. Just in time, I draw my attention to her rib cage, which is shallowly contracting upwards to draw in the stale air from the cellar for the final time. I watch as the carbonised air slips out of her partially open lips and vaporises into a fine ghost-like mist. It dissipates through the dimly lit cellar, then the tendrils of moisture curl momentarily around the ceiling light before disappearing into the thick darkness.

A quiet stillness has descended upon the room, an oddness caused by the absence of the expected inhalation, an interruption of the pattern that has captured my attention for the last fifteen minutes. Somehow the silence seems shocking to my mind, as if it cannot quite comprehend what I have just witnessed; the quiet moment of life slipping away into death. It is not what I was expecting, though what I had anticipated I cannot say.

For a brief moment, I feel nothing other than pure elation, my heart pumping with adrenaline as realisation strikes me that all my meticulous planning has paid off. Then the moment is gone. I was not expecting this deep cavernous emptiness that has so quickly replaced the joyous exaltation I had felt only seconds before, nor the terrible pain of loneliness that is now cutting deep into my soul with the awareness that I am now alone. I shiver, feeling cold despite the rivulets of sweat that are still pouring down the centre of my back. With the last feelings of elation passing, an exhausted numbness begins to spread throughout my limbs, leaving them feeling heavy and weak. My hands tremble at the sudden loss of adrenaline as it gradually drains away from them. I tuck my hands under my armpits, where the warmth from my labours soothes them back to life again.

The sudden movement of her upper body slumping to one side startles me. Fleetingly I wonder if somehow she is still alive, but a quick check of her pulse tells me that I am wrong. She is still dead. And I am still alone. How rapidly I have returned to that dark hole, where the light cannot penetrate through the omnipresent turgid gloom, where the air is fetid and stale and no matter how deep a breath I take, it will never be enough to satisfy the hunger in my lungs for fresh, clean air. The suddenness of the despair overwhelms me. I slide to the floor and sit cross-legged amongst the detritus that is now congealing and the urine that has been steadily seeping from her body, fanned out across the mattress.

It will not be long before rigor mortis starts to set in, I must get up again to resume my work. I push myself up off the floor, my hands sticky from the bodily fluids that have pooled at the edge of the mattress. Clumsily I try to pick up her floppy body but immediately drop her again. Seconds pass before my tired mind eventually deduces that I need to reach underneath her armpits and grab hold of the heaviest part of the *dead weight. With several jerky movements, I manage to haul her off the soiled mattress that has been her home for the past three days, and onto the cold cellar floor. As I drag her off the mattress, her heel catches on the piping around the edge. I crouch down to free the appendage and my hand touches something wet and viscous on the underside of her foot, where she has soiled herself. Without flinching I wipe my hands onto her stained and sodden dress, which had looked so pretty when she had first worn it.*

Sweat beings to pour down my spine again, I am tiring already and still have so much more work still to do. I drag her across the room, her head thumping rhythmically onto the hard concrete floor with every movement. Then somehow, I manage to find the strength to haul her up onto grandfather's wooden work bench and lay her out onto the tarpaulin that I have already pulled tightly across the wooden bench to protect it from damage. Her bodily fluids which continue to seep out of her, leave a dark, wet stain across the floor, leading a trail back to the mattress.

My tools are already laid out, lined up equidistant from each other, just as they have been for the past three days. Waiting to be used. The hand tools were once my grandfather's and I have been meticulous in my care of them since his passing. Of course, I have also added to the collection over the years, the creation of power tools has been a godsend and not an opportunity to be passed up.

Unlike most of the other properties in the road, the cellar to this particular house has electricity. An armoured electric cable runs from the mains in the kitchen and down the stairs, tacked onto the brick wall at regular intervals. The cable runs around the length of the room, neatly pinned to the brickwork until it reaches a double socket hanging above the bench.

Automatically I pick up my electric saw and plug it into one of the sockets. It switches on instantly with a whir, the noise filling the silent cavity. I take a deep breath and focus my mind on the task ahead.

Less than one hour later, the task is complete. Carefully I wrap the individual body parts up in the yellowing newspaper that I have found next to the kitchen aga. One by one, I take the packages up the rickety wooden stairs and into the tiny kitchen. Every time that I enter that room, I half expect to see my grandmother standing next to the cast-iron aga, cooking chicken stew and dumplings on top of the stove, a loaf of bread baking in the oven below. The aga was her pride and joy and she cleaned it every week without fail, even when she was panting for breath from the pneumonia that kept her in hospital for seven weeks before she finally died, her blue lips gasping from hypoxia. If only she could have shown me the same care and attention as she had shown to that aga, perhaps I would not be here now, clutching onto part of another human body, wrapped up tightly in old newspaper as if it were a large cod and chips from the fish and chip shop on the corner of the road.

The aga has been lit for the past three days, with the large stack of coal in the shed outside keeping it well fed. I wrap an old tea towel around the cast iron handle to shield my fingers from the depth of the searing heat, then open the aga door with a low screech that must surely be audible to the neighbouring property.

Reaching behind me, I pick up the topmost package from the pile on grandmother's kitchen table and throw the parcel into the fire. I watch as the package spits and crackles, flames enveloping the morsel that has just been thrown into its hungry jaws.

I watch as the flames devour the first of the nine

packages, then add another one, as if I am tending to a log fire whose smouldering embers need to be fed. In between each feed, I sit down in the old rocking chair in the corner of the room, where my grandmother would gently rock back and forth as she darned my school clothes. Rocking back and forth, I wait patiently for the flames to die down once more, before adding the next parcel into the aga. The quietness that has descended over the house is comforting. I watch the flames flickering through the cast iron door of the aga, which I have left open. The flames spit and crackle as they destroy the evidence that there had been another human being in this house. The sound soothes my soul as the flames cleanse me of the actions that I performed only a little while earlier.

When the is deed complete, I head back down into the cellar to begin to tidy up the mess that the girl has left on the floor and on the mattress, which is now heavily soiled and stained. A mop and bucket are already waiting next to the workbench and make light work of the congealed mess on the floor. There is little that can be done to resurrect the mattress, which I cover with the fresh bedlinen that I found earlier in the old pantry. I pull out a rag to clean the tools, ensuring that not one drop of blood remains, then soak the rag in oil and gently rub the metal blades with the liquid. The action reminds me of the moment when I looked into her eyes, that moment when she knew she was going to die. I have seen that look before, a long time ago when I was a curious child who saw things they should not have seen, standing in the cellar doorway when all the other good, obedient children were tucked up in bed asleep. I shake away the memory, this is not the time to be remembering what has passed. It is time to start planning for the future.

CHAPTER SEVEN

The newspaper drops onto the front door mat with its familiar thud. Silently I pull back the floral duvet, carefully placing my feet one at a time onto the floor below, taking care not to let the floorboards underneath the threadbare carpet creak. With both feet firmly planted on the carpet, I wait in quiet anticipation, listening for any movements within the house. Thirty seconds can feel like a lifetime when you are listening for the sound of footsteps, or of a bedroom door creaking open before being slammed against the wall behind it so hard that it makes a handle shaped dent in the brittle plaster. But there is only silence, the familiar sounds from my past are only in my mind's' eye.

Even so, I pull down the brass lever slowly, hoping that the movement will not be heard. As quietly as I can muster, I pull the door inwards and step out onto the landing, wincing as the floorboards involuntarily creak beneath my weight. I pause outside my bedroom door for a moment to stare at the door that leads to the large bedroom at the front of the house. I imagine the handle moving downwards, the door being slowly pulled back until there is an opening wide enough to allow a person to glide through. But it does not happen. The house is silent, except for the faint rhythmic ticking of that hateful clock penetrating softly through the floorboards from the room below.

Holding tightly onto the oak banister that wraps around the galleried landing before sweeping elegantly downwards in a half-turn, I gently patter down the stairs. My knees feel weak and I fear that they could give way and allow me to drop to the floor, but they hold up well enough for me to reach the bottom step, where I clutch onto the newel post as if it is a prize I have just won at the fair.

Lying prone on the light brown door mat is the daily local newspaper - The Suffolk Herald. I stoop down to pick it up then pad softly across the tiled hallway into the kitchen, where I flick on the pendulum light that hangs above the table. The bottom of the chair legs scrapes across the floor as I pull it back a little to allow enough room for me to squeeze in behind the table. Laying the paper onto the table, I carefully unfold it, smoothing out the pages, just as I did when I was a child, unwrapping a precious birthday present that would have cost my dad a week's wages. My heart thumps as I read the headline on the front page.

I run my tongue along my lips to moisten them a little as I read the article over and over again. There is something familiar about the girl's name, but I cannot recall why. What I do know though is that for some inexplicable reason, I am certain that what I am reading is of great significance to my life. I just do not know what it is.

I wonder who else might be sitting at their kitchen table, staring at the same article, whether the girl's parents have already seen their daughter's name in print. I wonder how they are feeling, knowing that their only child is missing. I wonder how it feels to have people who care.

Carefully I re-fold the newspaper, ensuring that the folds are in the same creases as before, then move across the hallway again to place it back onto the front door mat. I still recall the argument I had with Alex over the purchase of that door mat; it was not a necessity and was therefore considered to be a needless expense. I remember standing in the shop, picking it up, then putting it back down again on top of the other mats. I could not decide if purchasing would be worth the anguish that it was bound to cause. A week later I went back to the shop and when I returned home with the mat, wrapped up in a large brown paper bag, Alex did not speak to me again for nearly three days.

The stony silence of those three days weighed so heavily on my fragile mind that I never forgot how it made me feel. The guilt I suffered from the knowledge that it was I who had been the cause of the dense atmosphere that did not dissipate from the house for several weeks afterwards, was also a lesson that I never forgot. During that first week after the mat had been purchased, Alex was entirely absent. Every meal I cooked ended up in the bin, mugs of tea were left cold, sandwiches remained untouched on the dainty plates that once belonged to my mother. Gradually though, plates of food were emptied, cups of tea, drained. Then later, when I had conceded to remove the mat from where I had placed it next to the front door, I was eventually rewarded with a little polite conversation, only enough to aid the finding of freshly laundered trousers or to enquire if there was sufficient hot water in the tank for a bath, but still it was better than the stony silence that had prevailed. It was a long time though before normal conversation resumed and I have never bought anything without Alex's permission since.

Somewhere upstairs a floorboard creaks. I imagine Alex getting out of bed, ready to head towards the bathroom for a shower. Although it is imperative that money and resources are not wasted, it has also been instilled in me that cleanliness is a necessity to be prioritised. The shower can only be switched on though for exactly three minutes.

I must begin to assemble breakfast - lay out a bowl and spoon for cereal, accompanied by the stripy blue ceramic jug half-filled with milk, and a side plate of buttered bread. Next, I must place the matching egg holder onto the table, at equal distance between the edge of the table and the plate. The egg must be soft boiled for exactly two minutes and allowed to cool enough for the eggshell to be removed without searing delicate fingertips. As has become my habit of late, I have laid out the teapot and cups the previous night to quicken the process, the teapot always being in the centre of the table, the delicate cups and saucers at right angles, equidistant between the teapot and the plate.

I light the hob and place a pan of water over the flame and leave it to boil, then fill the kettle with the filtered cold water from the fridge, ready to switch on. I feel certain that the guilt I am feeling will be evident. I know that Alex's mother would never have done such a thing as to read a newspaper first. It was her belief that her husband's needs were always paramount. There are times when I seethe at the injustice of my being compared to someone who is so revered, knowing that I can never reach the pedestal that she has been placed upon. Occasionally a flicker of anger ignites, but it is quickly doused again for I understand that this is not the time to allow my emotions to rise up and rebel, but to allow them to simmer, and wait for the opportunity that I know one day will come.

I hear stair treads groan as if with displeasure at being trod upon. I flick the switch on the kettle and wait reluctantly with baited anticipation to discover what mood Alex will be in today.

'Good morning, Beth,' Alex says brightly.

I dare not look up, but instead stare transfixed at the kettle that is just beginning to boil. I cannot fathom if Alex is genuinely in a good mood or trying to lull me into a false sense of security, before beginning another tirade against any misdemeanors stored up that I might have inadvertently made.

'Would you like a cooked breakfast today as well as the cereal and boiled egg?' I ask hopefully, unable to hide the slight waver in my voice.

'Why are you asking me that?' Alex says quietly. 'You don't normally offer me a cooked breakfast. What have you done? Come on, I can hear the guilt in your voice.'

The colour immediately drains from my face. It is as if Alex can read my mind. There had been a time when I had thought this to be an endearing trait, but now it is my downfall, as my every move seems to be predicted.

'I haven't done anything,' I stammer, certain that my cheeks are now a deep crimson. With a trembling hand, I pour the boiled water into the teapot, then drop two teabags inside. The colourless liquid is rapidly infiltrated by the tea particles, turning it a golden brown that reminds me of the first leaves of the autumn. I am now confident that the tea has sufficiently brewed, so pick up the heavy vessel and pour the nectar into the awaiting cup, then pick up the delicate china and carefully traverse across the room to the table. I try to place the saucer down gently, but the contents slosh over the side, splashing onto the table below.

'I just thought you might be tired and want something extra to eat today,' I murmur, still staring at the spillage on the table, not daring to look up.

Alex snorts, the sound cutting through the thick atmosphere. I do not need to be told that I have angered Alex, I can tell from the stony silence that has fallen over the room.

My downcast eyes continue to watch as the sticky beige puddle travels outwards towards the edge of the table. I need to find a cloth to wipe up the mess, but I dare not move in case I do something else wrong. The noise from the omnipresent clock in the next room draws my attention away from the unbearable tension and for a moment I listen, comforted by the familiarity of the sound. By the time my focus returns to the kitchen again, I realise that there is now an absence of any other sounds. Alex has gone.

I almost miss the barely audible click of a front door being shut. The sound, which in years gone by I hated, I now welcome. That sound means I am alone. I can breathe once again.

Alex does not return until almost tea-time. As ever I am waiting in the hallway, sitting on the bottom step of the stairs, my worn slippers barely stemming the damp chill that rises up from the tiled floor. I pull my beige woolen cardigan a little more tightly across my torso, as much to provide me with comfort as for warmth.

The sound of a key turning in a lock stirs me from my quiet meditation and I move into the kitchen. Somewhere deep inside of me, I am clutching onto a faint glimmer of hope that perhaps Alex is in a more amenable mood than this morning, but my hopes are quickly dashed, going by the tense silence that has just fallen over the house.

Somewhere above me, a bathroom door slams shut, the door rattling in its wooden frame by the force of the action. Then the stillness of the house is interrupted by the sound of water steadily pulsating from an overhead shower into the bathtub below. The sound of running water quietens my mind. I listen to its regular rhythm intently until the sound of footsteps jolts me from my thoughts. My focus returns once more to the kitchen, where I am still sitting at the table. I stretch out each leg in turn, which are stiff from sitting for so long. Daylight is quickly receding and the house is beginning to darken. From my vantage point, opposite the hallway, I see shadows flickering on the wall next to the front door from the headlights of passing cars, no doubt their passengers are hurrying to reach home before the sun sets.

The darkness envelops me like a soft blanket as I traverse the room to stand in front of the stainless-steel sink and gaze through the window into the dark garden beyond. Subconsciously I grip onto the worktop, knuckles blanching as somewhere to the right of me a door slams open.

'I'm going out for a bit. When I get back, I expect you to look like how a woman is supposed to look.'

I try to bite back the tears, but I cannot stop them from forming under my tightly shut eyelids, nor can I prevent them from cascading down my cheeks. I do not turn around. I know that Alex is angry with me.

Seconds later a front door slams shut, stained glass windowpanes rattling with the force of the movement. I wince as the sound echoes through the quietness, imagining the reactions of the neighbours on the other side of the adjoining wall who must surely have heard it as loudly as if it had been their door.

I do not know what to do. My mind is filled with a mass of fear and confusion that swirls around the inside of my skull and will not allow even the tiniest of thoughts to form. I feel utterly lost. And alone.

I turn away from the window, suppressing the urge to run outside and never to return. Through the dim light, I spot a bottle on the worktop near to the sink. It is the bottle of Chardonnay that is to be saved for a special occasion. Yanking open the cutlery drawer, I quickly rummage through it, cutting my finger in my haste as I search for a corkscrew. My hands shake as I remove the wax that covers the cork and plunge the corkscrew in, twisting it hard. The corkscrew is released with a satisfying pop, which immediately calms my heart to a normal rate before I have even tasted the liquid. I know that Alex will be angry to discover that I have drunk it, but a small ember of rebelliousness is beginning to grow within me and at this present moment in time, I do not care what Alex thinks, or what punishment I will have to endure for such blatant disobedience.

I pour a large measure into one of the elegant wine glasses that my parents were given as a wedding present, then make my way to the table, pull out a chair and sit down heavily onto the wooden frame. As I gulp down the sweet liquid, I observe the warmth in the pit of my stomach, which rises upward towards the top of my throat. I cannot decide which sensation is the more satisfying, the numbing feeling from the alcohol that I am not used to consuming, or the sickly sharp pain in my abdomen from the acidity of the liquid that serves to remind me that I am still alive.

CHAPTER EIGHT

I spot her as soon as I turn right onto Landseer Road, a quarter of the way along the busy shopping street, just past the Pitt Stop café. Despite the late hour of the day, she is still in school uniform, wearing a dark grey knee length skirt and red striped shirt underneath a stone-grey cardigan. She looks so much like the others who have become part of my life journey, with her long chestnut hair, soft, round face and child-like eyes, glinting with innocence. Yes, it should be her. She will be my next one.

I check the wing mirror, flick on the indicator and pull over onto the double yellow lines to watch as she walks excitedly across the pavement at pace, a friend on either side of her, arms looped with hers. The three girls are chatting animatedly as they approach the corner shop at the end of the road. Something amusing is said and the girl in the middle throws back her head with laughter. She places a tiny hand onto the arm of the friend to the left of her and pushes her playfully, almost causing a collision with an elderly man who has just come out of the ironmongers. For a brief moment the girl looks back, gazing down the path that she has just walked up, her pearly white teeth flash across her angelic face. I know that smile is meant for me.

I continue to watch as the trio approach the corner shop. The girl in the middle clutches onto the money that her mother has given to her earlier, held securely within slender fingers that are tightly folded into a fist around the notes. The other hand, which is still placed upon the crook of her friends' arm, holds onto a purple velvet cloth bag, ready to carry home the shopping she has been asked to buy. She is a good girl, I can see it. She is pure and innocent. She is perfect.

I am so engrossed in watching the three girls as they walk through the open doorway and into the corner shop, that I do not notice the police car pulling up beside me until it has stopped in the middle of the road, blocking the main thoroughfare into town. I watch in the wing mirror as the officer straightens his hat, then steps out of the car. He pulls his jacket down as he walks across the road, ignoring the astonished occupants of the cars on either side, who can do nothing except wait. The traffic is beginning to build up already, a dozen curious faces peer out from their windows, trying to ascertain what is happening. I hardly dare to breathe as I wind down the window and turn to face the officer, a forced smile across my face, which I hope does not reveal my concern at this unexpected interruption.

'Can I help you Sir?'

'You're parked on a double yellow line….Sir.'

'I'm so sorry. I'm just waiting for my other half who's just gone to the shops. I'll move it now.'

The police officer tilts his head to the left and stares at me, brown eyes boring into me as if trying to read my mind. He opens his mouth to respond but his carefully prepared speech that precedes the systematic humiliation of hauling the unsuspecting occupant out of the car to be searched, is interrupted by the radio in his car crackling into life. He listens intently for a moment, then deduces that something more urgent requires his attention. The officer strides back out into the road, completely ignoring the inquisitive drivers who are still waiting patiently to go about their daily business, and clambers back into his car.

I watch out of the corner of my eye as he switches on the engine then speeds off in the direction of the town centre, rapidly followed by the line of cars who have been trapped behind him for the last few minutes. My eyes close involuntarily as I slowly exhale. I cannot believe my luck that just at that precise moment, something distracted him from searching my car. With my eyes still closed, I picture the dark brown roll bag nestled in the centre of the car boot. Inside the bag are all the tools I might need to carry out my plan. It must be a sign. I can feel it in my bones that this is all going to go exactly to plan. Exactly as I have imagined it.

Now all I can do is watch and wait for that perfect moment. The moment when she becomes mine. I slump down, nestling into the back of the torn leather car seat and smile at the thought. Imagining how the next scene will pan out. I allow myself an instant to savour the moment that will soon come, the exhilaration that I will be feeling when all my plans come to fruition. As I open my eyes again, the images in my mind fade away. I must be patient for the moment will come soon enough. But for now, I need to concentrate on the task ahead.

CHAPTER NINE

A sudden noise echoes through the house, awakening me from the deep slumber I have fallen into despite the ever-present feeling of fear that resides within me. It is a few moments before I can deduce the origin of the sound, and when I do, the familiarity of the sound of the kitchen door being opened, triggers a wave of emotion, convulsing through me as if I have had an electric shock. Alex.

Heavy footsteps are making their way upstairs, tripping up the steps two at a time, in a pattern that is ingrained on my soul. Shaking the last remnants of sleep from my exhausted mind, I frantically try to recall if I have placed the dressing table chair underneath the handle of the bedroom door, for it is the only way to secure it. I peer through the dark shadows, hoping against all odds to see the thick outline of a chair tilted at an angle, the top rail wedged up tightly underneath the door handle, but there is nothing there, except the grey, thin air that lays heavily across the room. I stare at the outline of the door which is now framed by the landing light penetrating through the linear gap around the outside of the wooden panel that has bowed and shrunken with age. I cannot move. Like a roe deer caught in the headlights of an approaching car, I am frozen with fear, sitting bolt upright on the crumpled bed covers. I pull up the crisp white top sheet that I had ironed only the previous day, underneath my chin and bury my face into the soft innocent material that smells of my childhood. Closing my eyes against what I know is about to occur, I repeat to myself, over and over again; 'please do not open the door, please do not open the door.'

Beads of sweat begin to form on the underside of my palms as my fingers clench tightly onto the sheet as if I am a toddler, clasping onto its security blanket. I shrink downwards into the bed, pulling the sheet up towards my head, wanting to become invisible, to become a ghost, to disappear. I am certain that my prayers will not be answered.

The silence shatters as the bedroom door is flung open so vehemently that the tarnished brass lever handle hits the stud wall behind it, making a dent in the dusky rose wallpaper that my mother had chosen for the room before I was born. I clamp my eyes shut even more tightly, not wanting to see the monster who I can sense is standing in the doorway. Pulling my clenched hands further up to cover my ears, I try to block out the heavy panting that has replaced my quiet breath.

'Don't be stupid,' a voice whispers in a measured tone, 'I know you're awake. C'mon then woman, do what you're supposed to do.'

The sound of breathing moves closer and as it does so, it becomes more laboured. Now there is a new sound, one of a leather belt being unstrapped, then slowly pulled through each trouser loop in turn before it is discarded onto the bare floorboards below. The sound of a zipper being pulled down, steel teeth forced apart until they have been fully separated, cuts through the thick silence that blankets the room. A foot stumbles and a hand is placed heavily onto the floral bedspread for support, as first one trouser leg is removed, then the other. The garment drops quietly onto the thin rug next to the bed. Then the bedspread that was once my mother's, is pulled back.

I cannot breathe. My mind has become numb. It is no longer part of a body that is now frozen into a catatonic state, lying prone along a cast iron double bed in a two-up, two down end terraced house, somewhere in the middle of the suburbs. I am no longer in my bedroom. I am far away. Somewhere safe.

Dawn breaks through the darkness and produces a warm orange glow that manages to penetrate through the heavy silence of my bedroom. The tense shadows on the wall opposite where I am lying, softly recede as the light gently pushes them away. Above the cacophony of the dawn chorus, a deep, gnarly rhythmic snore is resonating through the thin stud wall from the adjoining bedroom. An image comes to mind of my father, lying on his back, strewn diagonally across the bed, covers hanging off at one end of the bed, pillows askew. It was not often that my father drank to excess, but on the rare occasion that he did, he would invariably sleep in the front bedroom so as not to irritate my mother. Of course, this minor action could not suffice to placate my mother, who abhorred alcohol even more than she detested poverty, and she would not deign to talk to my father for several days on such an occasion.

The images fades as I gingerly swing my legs over the edge of the bed and place them gently onto the wooden floorboards. I test them one at a time to see if they can bear my weight without causing too much pain. It seems that my concern is unfounded as both appendages seem to work without causing too much distress. On the floor, next to my feet, is a brown leather belt; lying coiled up like a rattlesnake, ready to launch itself at my bare feet. I retch at the sight of it, the sounds of it being discarded by its owner the previous night, playing through my mind, over and over again.

Shivering I reach out for the plum-coloured velour fluffy dressing gown Alex insisted that I have last Christmas. It is lying neatly across the foot of my bed, on top of the disheveled, stained sheet. Tentatively I reach out to grab it, wincing at the movement. Ignoring the pain, I stretch my arm out farther until my efforts are rewarded by my fingers clasping onto the soft material. Pulling it towards me, I retrieve the heavy material and carefully pull it on, one arm at a time, then gently wrap it around me, pulling the belt around my waist so tightly that the cord cuts into my soft belly. I still remember the surprise that I had felt when Alex had chosen the gown, it was such rarity to be allowed such a luxurious item. This seemingly innocuous item had been a small beacon of light in the darkness that was smothering my life. Now it will only serve to remind me of what occurred last night.

Gingerly I place my full weight onto my feet and pull myself up, trying to ignore the red-hot pain that is searing deep inside my pelvic cavity. I pause for a moment and take several deep, steady breaths, concentrating on the process of inhaling and exhaling, until the wave of pain subsides. The bedroom door now seems such a great distance to travel that I have to will myself on towards it. The dark oak stained floorboards creak ominously as I tip-toe across them, the noise leaving me fearful that I will be heard. My heart is thudding so strongly against my bruised ribs from the exertion, that I have to stop to breathe away the pain. I close my eyes to concentrate, breathe in, breathe out. Just keep breathing.

With my heart rate slowing again, I decide to continue on my journey. I creep towards the bedroom door that is still partially open, in the same position where it has been left only a few hours ago. I fight back another wave of nausea that is rising from the pit of my stomach. I cannot think about last night now. I need to concentrate on the task ahead.

Gently I push the door open a little wider, so that I can fit through it without touching it. I fight to stifle a soft groan as the pain between my legs becomes stronger and stronger with every step that I take. As I traverse the landing and begin to descend the staircase, I can still hear the resoundingly repetitive eruptions coming from the direction of the front bedroom. After every creak of the wooden steps, I pause for a moment and listen. The absence of any movement other than mine, reassures me and my confidence begins to grow with every raspy rattle that is emitted. Silently I bargain with myself, making a pact with any higher force that may exist, that if the monster in the front bedroom does not wake up, I will be the kindest, most loving person anyone could ever be from now on. Emotions choke in the top of my throat as I hope against all hope that the mantra will keep me safe for a little while longer. It did not work last night.

As I reach the half-turn of the staircase, the weak rays of the emerging sun are just beginning to shine through the stained-glass front door, making the yellow and orange panes glow, as if they are on fire. The light casts elongated shadows along the terracotta stone floor, which always stays cold, regardless of the time of year. The dark shape reminds me of a band of stone sentries, standing guard at the graveside of some long-forgotten king. Fleetingly I wonder what has happened to Merlin, the shadow who is always beside me.

I reach the bottom tread, step over the section that creaks, then place both feet firmly onto the floor below. Immediately I regret that I have not had the presence of mind to bring my slippers, which are still sitting on the rug next to my bed - by the time I reach the open sitting room door, my feet are as frozen and numb as my heart.

I peer into the sitting room, which is encased in darkness; the heavy curtains are still closed and block out the daylight that is starting to increase in strength. As I pass by the open doorway, there is a dull thud behind me. The noise startles me and I feel a small trickle of urine run down my left leg. I close my eyes bracing myself for what is to come, but the house remains quiet, aside from the ticking of the clock on the mantlepiece. Forcing myself to open my eyes again, I pluck up the courage to turn around and seek out the cause of the sound. It is just the morning newspaper, that is now lying motionless across the front door mat. Exhaling forcefully, I shuffle back up the hallway and stoop down to pick it up, in the full knowledge that I will suffer Alex's wrath for such a blatant disobedience, but the need to diminish the ever-present sense of impenetrable isolation, is greater than my fear of any punishment that I might endure.

Placing the newspaper onto the small mahogany hallway table, I carefully flip it open so that the front page is uppermost. The headlines of the main news article immediately catch my attention.

SUFFOLK HERALD

Another Local Girl Goes Missing

Another girl has gone missing, leaving the whole town reeling in shock at yet another unexplained disappearance. The parents of Caitlyn Field have confirmed that their daughter was last seen on Saturday morning after going to the local shops with her friends. The fourteen-year-old, Fairfield School student did not return home after purchasing milk and eggs at a shop on the High Road nearest to their home. Mrs Field has confirmed that Caitlyn has never run away before and that her disappearance is completely out of character.

Dog Photo Competition

The annual winter dog photographic competition will be held indoors this year due to expected inclement weather. Anyone wishing to take part in the competition should contact Debbie Reid on 222777 for more information about how to enter their pets. Prizes for the show have been donated by local business and include a free meal for two at the towns new bistro.

I have barely read the headline, when I realise that the sound of snoring upstairs has stopped. Quickly I place the newspaper back onto the coarse door mat and pad softly into the kitchen, where I begin to make breakfast, just the way Alex has taught me. Just the way Alex's mother used to do.

As I drop two eggs into a pan of water that has just boiled, my mind flits back to the newspaper headlines. There is something in the back of my mind niggling at me, but I cannot quite grasp what it is. Perhaps I do not wish to know. Perhaps it is a memory that I have locked away in the attic of my mind and I do not wish to locate the old, heavy key to open that door again. Still, it is now there and once acknowledged, cannot be unseen. A seed has been planted in my mind that one day will grow and take hold, refusing to be ignored any longer, determined to be heard. But for now, I will lock those thoughts safely away again for another time.

The realisation that it is Monday strikes me. Alex will soon leave. I can almost feel the sense of relief already, that I know will wash over me as soon as the front door clicks shut. There is a small voice inside of me that says this cannot be what other people feel when the person they love is absent. But if that voice is wrong and this is all there is in life for me, then I have nothing else to hope for. Hope is not something that I dare to contemplate and it is dangerous for me to do so, for if I begin to hope and fail, then I will be in a much worse position than I am now.

The kitchen door opens, releasing me from my thoughts in an instant as I feel two eyes boring into me. It is Merlin who always seems to know when I need him.

'Hello Merlin,' I say, stooping down to stroke the soft fur on the top of his head. I massage his temples the way he has always enjoyed and am rewarded by a soft, raspy purr that interjects the silence, giving me a moments relief from the fear that is slowly crushing me.

Merlin begins to rub up and down against my legs, leaving a trail of dark fur splattered on my bare skin. I know when the feline needs feeding and quickly locate a tin of food at the back of the cupboard. Scraping some of the meat onto a clean saucer, I place it near the back door and stand back, awaiting the prince to fulfil his nutritional needs. But it seems that this time I am wrong, for Merlin saunters past me and squeezes through the opening of the door, which is slightly ajar. A jolt of fear hits me like a thunderbolt. The back door is open.

I am still there, staring at the open door when I hear a voice sigh loudly. A gentle cough to clear the throat tells me that Alex is annoyed. I do not dare to look up as I return to the worktop to continue with the breakfast preparations. Carefully I place the teapot, cup and saucer onto a tray, then locate a cereal bowl, the Tupperware box of muesli and the milk that I have already poured into the cream ceramic jug that was given to my parents as a wedding present. My hands are slippery with sweat as I carry the tray and place it in the centre of the table. Then I relocate each item from the tray to the table, just as I have been taught.

I still do not dare to look up but instead focus on the task ahead of me. Even so, I can feel eyes watching me as I pick up the tray to replace it on the worktop again. Tears cascade down my cheeks as I try to decide if I should look or not. If I do, I could be chastised for the action, if I remain as I am, that too may be held against me. Damned if I do. Damned if I do not. I cannot decide what would anger Alex the least at this present moment. Instead, I screw my eyes up tightly to try to stem the flow of tears that are running down my cheeks.

'What have I told you about ignoring me?' Alex yells so loudly that the noise frightens me and I feel a slight trickle of urine run down my leg. I pray that it goes unnoticed.

'It's fucking rude, isn't it?'

I nod my head veraciously, my hair whipping across my cheeks, several strands becoming plastered to my jowl by my tears and your saliva. The thought of bodily fluid on me makes me nauseous and I fight to control the stomach acid that has risen involuntarily into the top of my throat.

'So', Alex says, drawing out each syllable slowly in a quiet voice that is reserved for the worst of my misdemeanors. 'You know that you need to be punished.'

I cannot hold myself back any longer. The trickle of tears becomes a torrent, sticky droplets cling onto my eyelashes momentarily before they flood down my cheeks and drip off the end of my nose, adding to the humiliation I already feel at having so little control over my own body. I know that this will be another black mark against me.

The chair scrapes across the kitchen floor as it is pushed back with such force that it hits the wall behind. I am suddenly aware of a burning pain in my wrist, which feels as if my skin is on fire. I shuffle out of the kitchen and into the hallway, my elbow hitting the door handle in the process. I know where I am going and can no longer prevent the tears from cascading uncontrollably down my cheeks, my shoulders jerking so hard that I feel as if I will collapse with pain. For a split second I consider whether I can escape. But it is too late. The moment is now over and all I can do is wait meekly for the key to be retrieved from where it is kept under the carpet of the seventh step. The door to the cupboard underneath the stairs is unlocked and pulled open, releasing a cloud of stale air from the cavern within. I cannot breathe. I know what my punishment will entail. I have been there before.

CHAPTER TEN

The girl is so completely engrossed in conversation as she hurries out of the shop, that she does not notice there is someone sitting in the driver's seat of a dark blue Ford Fiesta that is parked over the double yellow lines. Nor does she notice the car pull out in front of the oncoming traffic to follow her as she waltzes down the pavement, arm in arm with her friends, talking animatedly about something that has just happened.

The girl in the centre of the group, with blond hair pulled back into neat pigtails, turns her head around to glance back up the path that leads to the corner shop she has just left. My eyes follow her gaze and immediately I spot two young males stepping through the shop doorway and out into the low afternoon sun. The girls huddle together more closely, giggling loudly. Another glance back towards the shop makes it obvious that they are talking about the boys, who are now walking behind them a few feet away, pretending to be uninterested in them.

One of the lad's glances in my direction, an expression of mild curiosity on his face at the car that is still moving slowly along the road. He looks away again, his interest being held more keenly by the trio of females in front of him. The lad runs forward to catch up with the girl with the pigtails, pulling her roughly to one side. Seconds later, with her friends momentarily forgotten, her arms are thrown around his neck, pulling him towards her for a kiss. As soon as their lips touch, she playfully pushes him away again. He throws up his arms in mock annoyance, knowing only too well that it is all a game and eventually she will concede to his persistent advances. But for now, the moment has passed and he will not get to further his limited experience of sexual encounters on this occasion.

The boys allow the distance between them and the girls to lengthen before suddenly turning off the High Road by taking a left turn onto Quilter Road. At first their absence is unnoticed, but when it is noted, the girl with the pigtails pulls an overly dramatic mock sad face, before laughing loudly. She too knows how to play the game. She will not give in too easily though, however much she wishes to, for her mother has drummed it into her that once she has given up what is being sought, the boy will have no further use for her and will discard her for the next conquest.

The car remains unnoticed by the three girls when they finally part company at the end of the road, still engrossed in re-enacting the scene that has just taken place - one that has marked another milestone in their journey into adulthood. Now the girl with the pigtails is alone, left to complete the remainder of the short journey without the security of her friends. The time has come.

I accelerate down the road a little to overtake the girl, then pull over to the side of the road a little way ahead of her. I have watched this journey of hers so many times already that I am certain of the path she will take towards home. Right on cue, she appears in my rear-view mirror. I wait until she is almost level with the car, then wind down the driver's side window.

'Excuse me, do you know how to get to the

cinema?'

'Sure, you'll need to carry on down the end of this road, turn left then take a right, you can't miss it.'

Just as she finishes giving directions, the heavens open, unleashing a torrent that immediately begins to overwhelm the gutters that the council have not yet cleared as part of their annual maintenance cycle. The girl shrieks, pulling up the collar of her denim jacket underneath her ears, but it does little to shield her from the deluge that is now running down the path, across the kerb and into the overflowing drains.

'Can I give you a lift, it looks like we're going the same way?'

'Thank you so much!' she says without a moment's hesitation. She flips a bird at the car behind me, who is beeping its horn in annoyance that I am blocking the lane in front of them. She steps out into the road and pulls open the passenger side door that I have pushed open a little for her. With a cursory glance inside to make sure she is not stepping onto anything lying in the footwell, she throws herself into the front seat and slams the door shut.

'This is so kind of you, I live near the cinema so can show you where it is.' The girl chatters excitedly.

'You're very welcome. I couldn't just leave you out in the rain like that, especially as you were kind enough to help me. What's your name?'

'Caitlyn,' the girl beams at me. She places her sodden bag of shopping into the footwell then reaches behind her to pull across the seatbelt. I help her to clip it securely into place, then check the rear-view mirror before pulling out into the traffic.

'What music do you like Caitlyn?'

'Oh lots, I like Wham, Boy George, Bananarama.'

I smile at her, then reach over to turn the knob on the radio, brushing against her right knee in the *process. She moves away from me a little and places her hands on top of her skirt, smoothing it down until the creases caused by the rain have dissipated. Flicking through the tuner, I find a local station that plays the sort of pop music the girl likes, then place my hand back onto the wheel, allowing my fingers to drum on the leather in time to a song that is playing.*

The girl relaxes back into the chair, stretching her long, slender legs out in front of her, her toes pressed up against the side of the shopping bag. The song ends and the DJ announces the next tune. As it begins to play, she sings along to it softly. I cannot help but smile, this is going so much better than I could ever have imagined.

At first, she does not notice that we have not turned into Clerkenwell Street, she is still too engrossed in the song that is clearly one of her favourites. Out of the corner of my left eye, I watch as she begins to realise that we have missed the turning.

'Hey, we've gone past it, you'll need to turn around as this road goes out to the other side of town.'

'Don't worry, I know a short-cut.'

She looks puzzled, unsure of how to respond. She snuggles back down into the chair again with less certainty than before. Slowly I move my right hand onto the door handle, and gently squeeze the central locking button, hoping that the radio will disguise the sharp click. The sound does not go unnoticed.

'Hey what are you doing? Pull over, I want to get out.'

'Sorry Caitlyn but I'm afraid I cannot do that.'

'Why not?'

As soon as the words leave her mouth it dawns on her that something has changed. She is no longer a passenger catching a lift home. She is my prisoner.

I reach down into the top of my boot, where I have

secreted a short, stubby knife. The movement does not go unnoticed and suddenly Caitlyn reaches for the door handle, pumping it up and down with such force that I fear it will break.

'Don't be stupid now, I have a knife here and am prepared to spoil your pretty face if I need to.'

The words have their desired effect. She curls up into a ball, rounding her back into the chair, hands clasped around her head, emitting large gasping sobs that leave her unable to breathe. She does not move again. The only inkling that she is still alive is from her rapid breathing, which has become less laboured the further we travel from the town centre. She is already learning acceptance.

Dusk is falling by the time we reach the far end of town. In silence we pass through the new suburb of detached houses, whose spacious gardens mean that occupants are no longer forced to make polite conversation with their neighbours as they enter and leave their homes. The tree lined estate gives way to row upon row of red-brick terraces, where the houses are crammed together and the only greenery comes from the graffiti covering the boarded-up window on the corner shop. We meander through the narrow, deserted streets, where residents hide behind closed curtains and the children in their second-hand shoes, play in the streets on their worn out bikes until the light fades into night. At the far end of the estate, most of the houses are in a state of disrepair, and the occupants who live on the other side of the boarded-up windows, choose to spend their benefits down the pub instead of keeping their children warm. It is a place where an old tin bucket is always kept under the stairs for when it rains, and the black mould that covers the metal window frames, creeps up the corners of the children's bedroom walls, that are *plastered in thin magazine posters depicting bands they have watched on TV.*

We pass through a labyrinth of worlds that are far removed from where Caitlyn has been brought up; with her long-forgotten dapple-grey pony and the girl's school that failed to teach her about the dangers of getting into a stranger's car. I cannot help but wonder if the girl sitting next to me would be here at all if she had attended the local comprehensive and become as streetwise as her poorer peers.

The light has almost entirely faded by the time I pull over kerbside at the back of Ivry Street. The streets are empty, the children have gone home for their tea of sausage and chips if they are lucky, or for those less fortunate, a bowl of cereal that would have to suffice to keep the hunger pangs at bay during the long winter night. As always, my timings have been planned impeccably and by the time we park, there is no one else in the street to see me guiding a frightened teenage girl through the dank passageway towards the gate that leads to the back yard of number 6 Ivry Street.

CHAPTER ELEVEN

It feels as if hours have passed since I last saw daylight. My back aches from crouching down in such a small space, my knees are stiff and sore from being bent into the same position. My mouth is so dry from lack of water that I cannot even moisten my cracked lips. Even if my parched throat would allow me to, I know that it is futile to call out. I will not be heard. I have tried before.

Locked in the darkness, time loses all perspective. I could have been here for thirty minutes or three hours and I would not know the difference. I know from previous punishments that after a while the sterility of the quiet darkness begins to play tricks with the mind. No sounds from the outside world can penetrate through the thick planks of wood that comprise the cupboard; noises that could have provided some comfort to me and served as a reminder that there are other people nearby. Sounds that would have made me feel less alone.

Time drifts without the anchor of familiar noises to keep a person in the present; the dawn chorus that heralds the breaking of the morn; the familiar whirr of the milk float as it stops outside the front of the house at 6am to collect the empty bottles from the doorstep and replace them with fresh ones; the quiet thud of the newspaper dropping onto the front door mat that tells you it is now 7.30am, and not long afterwards, the sound of people getting into their cars, doors slammed in haste and engines switched on as they hurry off to work, and later, the reverse as they return to their homes after a long day at work. But the only noise inside the cupboard is the regular rhythm of my shallow breathing as I try to glean what is left of the ever-depleting supply of oxygen in the warm, stale air.

Nor is there anything that I can feast my eyes upon to distract me. The impenetrable blanket of darkness is interjected only by a sliver of yellow light that encompasses the edge of the shiplap cladding encasing the staircase. I cannot tell if it is daylight or if the light is coming from the warm glow of the reproduction Tiffany lamp that sits at one end of the console table next to the front door. It is as if time is standing still, that my life is on hold until that moment when the door opens again.

The first time I was punished in this way I had panicked. Sitting next to the squat timber door that has been painted white to blend in with the cladding on the staircase, I had slapped my hands against the wooden panels until they were sore. The sharp noise reverberating around the empty space was as shocking in the silence as if a gun had been fired within the cramped space. The noise had been too much for my tortured mind to bear and broke the spell that I had been under. The frantic need to escape had evaporated into an air of submission as I slumped against the door, waves of exhaustion and despair washing over me. I recall how I had sobbed so vehemently that a torrent of nausea had risen up from the pit of my empty stomach, which was by now filled only with the acids that were eating away at the lining in desperation. All of my pathetic attempts to communicate with the outside world had ended in failure. For on the other side of the door there was only silence, except of course for the omnipresent ticking of the carriage clock that sits pride of place in the centre of the mantelpiece in the front sitting room.

Even now, that moment still intrigues me, the discovery of pure gratitude that one feels when even the smallest of comforts have been taken away from them. How precious the most basic of needs become when they are no longer within our remit. I recall how on that first occasion, I had indignantly squatted in the far corner of the cupboard out of desperation to relieve myself. I knew that I could be punished for such an action but I could not bear the discomfort a moment longer. However, I was not punished, not then in any case. It was later, when I became re-acquainted with the cupboard for the second time, that I discovered that I was not to be allowed even the most meagre amount of water. This harsh lesson had been saved for the summer months, when the stifling heat becomes trapped inside this wooden coffin making it difficult to breathe. I also discovered, that after a while the lack of oxygen, coupled with dehydration, causes the person to feel so ill that they fear they will not survive whilst coupled with the overwhelming desire for unconsciousness to rescue you even if you never woke again. In the depths of winter, the cupboard provides a different lesson, when the bitter cold from the terracotta floor tiles freezes the lower portion of the body to such an extent, that even sitting in a bath of scalding water cannot easily redress the excruciating numbness encasing the lower part of the body. Of course, it may have helped if sufficient depth of water were allowed, but rules must always be adhered to and even in these most desperate of times, disobedience is not permitted.

On those first occasions, I had not known how to endure the punishment. I still recall the weight of silence laying heavy in the small space, the blanket of fear which crushed me into a blithering creature who could do nothing but sob at the injustice of the situation. Eventually I learnt to calm myself. I imagined myself somewhere else, back on the beach from my childhood, a sanctuary away from the despair and pain that was overwhelming my life. I have become so adept at visualisation, that I could actually feel the cool air from the wind whipping across the sea and up the beach against my weary face; the heat from the sun's heavy rays filling me with hopeful energy again; the waves crashing onto the shingle shore, soothing my tired mind.

Now I have even come to embrace this time of solitude and reflection, to find comfort in the darkness as an accepting calm washes over me. For even though I do not know how long I will be there, I now know that at some point I will be released. It is this thought alone that my sanity clings onto during the long hours, the knowledge that the door will open, allowing light and fresh air to flood in with a bittersweet feeling of gratitude that I am able to leave the cupboard, coupled with a fear of the unknown in doing so. Of late, the cupboard has transformed from my prison to my place of safety, just as Alex who was once the protector I revered and trusted to keep me safe from harm, has become an intrepid stranger to be feared.

Today though, my mind is a deep void of nothingness. There is little I can do to distract myself when even my imagination has deserted me. My mind cannot focus on the merest semblance of a lucid thought that could transport me away from the dingy, cramped space and out into the wide-open space of the beach I had loved so much as a child. It is as if my soul can no longer endure my existence and has departed, perhaps never to return. At this moment in time, I am a ghost. I feel nothing and no longer care if I am alive or dead. I cannot even summon the presence of mind to consider if death would be a way to escape from this infinite misery. So, I sit, with the top of my head resting against the internal wooden struts of the staircase, my back pressing into the rough-shorn upright timbers that hold up the staircase above me and wait for my punishment to end.

The sharp audible click of the deadlock on the front door being released, brings my focus back to the present. The squeak of hinges that need to be oiled, solidifies my thinking that Alex has returned. I try to make myself look more presentable, pulling at the hem of my top to straighten it a little, folding down the collar which has ridden up towards my ears. I run my fingers through my wavy auburn hair. Then I sit and patiently wait.

The first time I was punished it had felt like an eternity until the moment I was released. I had sat motionless underneath the stairs, hearing footsteps moving above me, followed by the sound of a bath being filled, accompanied by muffled humming. Whilst I sat in my urine-soaked trousers, a seed of doubt began to grow in my mind that I could have been forgotten. The fear that filled me at the thought of dying alone in the darkness, was almost unbearable. I did not dare cry out in case I angered Alex and had instead sobbed uncontrollably into my hands that I placed over my face to block out the confusing world I had found myself in. My fears of course were unfounded, the cupboard door was duly opened and I clambered out. Vividly I recall not being allowed to wash or change my sodden clothes until I had made a mug of strong tea, with one sugar and only a splash of semi skimmed milk, then grilled the pork chops the butchers' new lad had delivered to the house that morning. Those early memories now seem a lifetime ago. The shock of the punishments soon dissipated as the new normality quickly took hold and I adapted once again to my new life.

This time the wait is a short one. The door opens to reveal the artificial light from the ceiling light in the hallway, for daylight has already come and gone.

'Have you had a good day?' Alex says quietly.

'Yes', I respond meekly as I try to climb out of the cupboard with as much dignity as I can muster from my stiff limbs.

'Why don't you have a quick bath before supper?'

I smile weakly, not daring to speak, hoping that my eyes do not betray the confusion I am feeling at this unexpected kindness. I cannot decipher the reasoning behind it. Perhaps Alex has had a good day and has decided to show some compassion, which would be out of character, but not impossible. Or perhaps a further punishment awaits me and I am now being lulled into a false sense of security. I cannot bear to consider the second option. I am not ready to go back there again. Not yet.

The bath is so warm and comforting that my heavy eyes involuntarily close. The warmth of the water reminds me of the over-sized lilac blanket my mother would tuck around me in the winter months, as I sat in an armchair in front of the open fire in the sitting room.

How I wish that I never have to leave the safety of this liquid cocoon, with its comforting, intoxicating familiarity that entices me to stay. Reluctantly though I open my eyes and focus on the soft tendrils of steam that are winding their way up to the ceiling before curling around the ceiling light above me. I am mesmerised by the steam as it rises, frozen in a dream like state from which it seems I cannot wake.

It takes every ounce of resolve that I can muster to heave myself up out of the tub, droplets of water splashing onto the bathroom floor in the process. I grab hold of one of the coral-coloured towels from the rail, drop to my knees and dab at the pink, short-pile carpet. I feel my stomach tighten at the thought that Alex might find out about the sodden carpet. I seem to be doing so much wrong of late, that I live in a perpetual state of fear, never knowing if I am going to anger Alex or not. I do know though that it is not possible for Alex to be more disappointed in me than how I already feel about myself.

I cannot put it off any longer, it is time to leave this warm, safe space. As I pull on a fresh pair of trousers and fasten the white shirt Alex chose for me for my last birthday, I catch sight of myself in the full-length mirror that is fixed to the wall next to the door. I have not looked at myself for so long that I barely recognise the drab, gaunt figure staring back at me, with her rounded back and sagging shoulders. Is that really me? Is that what I have become? No wonder Alex feels such disdain towards me. I can now understand why I cannot be seen in public. I would feel ashamed to been seen with me as well. How will I ever face the world again, now that I know how pathetic I have become?

There is something that seems oddly familiar about the ludicrous creature standing opposite me. For a moment I cannot recall what I am being reminded of and stare at the figure before me, taking in every part of the emaciated frame and dull, lifeless eyes. Then, a memory flashes into my mind of a trip to Crete many years ago with mother, the year after my father died. It was the first time either of us had ever been abroad and we had been overwhelmed by the tranquil beauty of the island and the warmth of the local people who served us cocktails every night at the piano bar on the beach. There was one other memory though that I have never forgotten, one that has pricked at my conscience years after the holiday was over, it was of the stray dogs who gathered at the back of the taverns every evening, hoping for a few scraps of food to keep them alive a little longer, their ribs jutting out from their concave bodies, heads bent low in submission, a flicker of hope in their eyes that perhaps they might be shown some token of kindness. But it is the bruises on their backs from the stones the tavern owners pelted at them to shoo them away before the tourists could see them, that has been forever etched into my mind. And the fact that they returned to the tavern's night after night in mournful desperation, knowing that they would be chased away again. It is of them that I am now reminded of when I look in the mirror. I close my eyes and turn away in disgust. I cannot bear to look at this pathetic creature in front of me any longer.

CHAPTER TWELVE

She has been with me now for three days. At first, she had simply sat in the corner of the cellar and cried. Each time I approached, her hands, still bound at the wrists, were promptly flung over her face and I could not have prised them away without breaking her fingers. If I tried to touch her, she had flinched, her shoulders shaking involuntarily, belying the fear she was trying to keep hidden deep inside.

On the morning of the second day, I had carefully made my way down the steep steps holding a melamine tray in my right hand, my left clutching onto the rickety banister. The girl had watched my every move, from where she was sitting in the centre of the filthy, sagging mattress that has been pushed back against the wall nearest to the staircase. She was beginning to relax a little, her confidence growing under the false assumption that was forming in her mind, that as nothing bad has happened to her so far, perhaps it was not going to. She underestimated me.

As I placed the plate of ham sandwiches onto the floor in front of her, she looked into my eyes for the first time, a tentative thin-lipped smile appeared, revealing her newly formed adult canines, gleaming brightly against the darkness of the brick wall behind her. I took a step back and watched as she grabbed hold of the plate and began to nibble at the corner of one half of the sandwich. She was starting to believe she was safe.

On the third day, the dynamics of our relationship altered dramatically. Just as I did the day before, when I entered the cellar, I placed a bowl of steaming hot porridge drizzled with a little honey in front of the girl. I took a step back, expecting to be rewarded by some small token of gratitude, but she was cunningly deceiving me with her pretence of amicableness. The reward for my kindness was to kick the bowl away with a clatter. The vessel rolled across the concrete floor until it landed, upturned at the bottom of the staircase. I barely managed to contain the anger that was welling up inside of me at her insolence. I turned to look at her and was met with a glare of defiance that revealed to me the deliberateness of her actions. She felt certain that she was safe.

As with a toddler who was testing their boundaries, I did not acknowledge her misdemeanour, but instead, turned my back on her and began to clear up the mess made from the porridge, which had glopped onto the concrete floor and was beginning to congeal onto the rough concrete surface. The calm demeanour I exuded hid the anger that was beginning to bubble up inside of me at the impedance of her actions. My mind was filled with a jumble of questions as I tried to understand why she was behaving in this way. Did she not understand all that I had done for her? Saving her from the life that had been mapped out before her, perpetuating the same cycle of teenage motherhood, abuse and misery as the other girls? Did she not realise how special she was, that she had been chosen? She had repaid my kindness by *behaving like a spoilt toddler who did not wish to eat their breakfast,*

Steeling myself not to react, I did not acknowledge her as I carried the battered stainless-steel bowl up the stairs again, nor did I say my customary 'goodbye' when I turned out the ceiling light, plunging her into darkness. The girl did not know this, but my silence portrayed the severity of the anger that I felt inside, for my quiet demeanour belies when I am at my most vengeful. Soon she would learn a very valuable lesson as a result of her actions, as I have learnt that I cannot trust her.

There was only silence in the cellar when I had shut the door and roughly pulled the bolt across, fixing the padlock with a sharp click that would be audible in the room below. I imagined her sitting in the centre of the filthy mattress in the darkness, wondering what I was planning to do next. Not for one moment did I think that she was foolish enough to believe that I would do nothing to punish her rebelliousness.

And so it is that I have come to be sitting in the kitchen in the dark, waiting. For the longer I wait, the higher her cortisone levels will rise at a similarly proportional rate to her rapidly depleting confidence levels. Now it has become a battle of wills, and this is a fight I will not lose.

Dawn is rising above the roofline of the block of terraced houses that are perpendicular to the alleyway that runs along the bottom of the garden of 6 Ivry Street. The house is silent, no sounds have been emitted from the cellar during the six hours that I have sat at the small rectangular table, in what would have been total darkness had it not been for the light from the crescent moon cutting through the impenetrable gloom. There has been no whimpering or crying, no pleading for an end to the darkness that will have weighed heavily on her mind. For a fleeting moment I wonder if she is still alive, but I resist the urge to check up on her. My curiosity will be satisfied soon enough.

On top of the small blackened aga in the back living room, I gently warm some porridge, taking care to stir it frequently so that it does not burn the bottom of the pan. I have already laid out two bowls on the table, stainless steel spoons resting beside them. I watch the off-white concoction as it begins to bubble, then switch off the stove. Using a tea towel from the table, I take hold onto the scorching cast iron handle of the heavy saucepan and pour the gloopy mixture equally into the two bowls. The task complete, I sit back down on the chair that I have occupied for the entire night and eagerly consume the contents of one of the bowls. The other bowl is almost cold by the time I finish eating, but this is not my concern. She should be grateful to receive any nourishment regardless of its condition.

Gingerly I stand up, my knees stiff from the many hours of sitting motionless. Picking up the untouched spoon and the bowl containing the remaining porridge, I make my way across the room towards the hallway. The door to the cellar is housed underneath the staircase, the orangey-pine panelling hiding the entrance to the room below from any curious eyes. With my unoccupied hand, I slide the key that I have retrieved from my trouser pocket, into the keyhole, twist the metal shaft until I hear a satisfying click, then remove it before sliding it back into my trousers. I unclip the padlock and pull the bolt across, noting the ease of the movement after the oiling I gave the mechanism last weekend. I am *certain that the familiar dull creak of the door opening will not have gone unnoticed in the room below.*

I pause at the top of the stairs. Placing the palm of my hand flat against the wall, I carefully slide it across the rough bricks until the corner of a plastic light switch makes contact with my fingers. With a sharp click, the ceiling light flicks on. I watch for a moment, as the uncovered lightbulb that is fixed to the underside of the struts from the kitchen floor above, sways gently in the centre of the room like a pendulum at a hypnotists' stage show.

The girl is still sitting in the centre of the mattress, legs dangling over the edge, bare feet planted prone onto the cold, concrete floor. She does not look at me as I descend the staircase, taking care to avoid the step that is third from the bottom and is beginning to rot in the damp atmosphere. Nor does she look at me when I place the bowl of porridge at her feet. This time she does not kick it away, but sits rigidly, her head bowed in submission. I can see the uncertainty she is feeling, wrestling with herself, not knowing what she should do. As the minutes tick by, the porridge is beginning to congeal into an unappetising mass.

'I see that you are not hungry today,' I say, stooping down to collect the bowl from the floor. Standing upright, I place the spoon into the vessel and quickly eat the contents, ignoring the sharp intake of breath that comes to the right of me.

Without even the merest of glances in her direction, I turn my back on the girl and stride over to the far end of the room towards grandfather's bench. I place the now empty bowl at the far end of the bench and methodically begin to take down each of the tools from where they are hanging on metal pegs fixed into the brick wall. A cleaning cloth and oil are already waiting on the bench, in the same place they have always been kept. The familiarity of the process soothes me. Carefully I clean each tool in turn then hold it up to the spotlight lamp to check the quality of my work, before laying it out, exactly 15cm from the nearest tool.

I do not need to turn around to know that the girl is watching, I can sense that she is. Another sharp intake of breath tells me that I am correct in my thinking. I glance at my watch, the illuminous hands glowing in the dim light. It is time for the lessons to begin. The girl has a lot to learn and I have a lot to teach her. Perhaps soon she might like a companion, someone to keep her company and help her with her lessons? I smile to myself at the thought. What an excellent idea, I cannot believe I did not think of it before. I will begin my search today.

CHAPTER THIRTEEN

The house has been quiet for weeks. At first the silence had felt eerie and I had solemnly grieved the loss of my companion, detesting the fact that I had been left alone once again. But in time, Alex's absence has allowed my mind to process all that has happened to me since mother died. It seems as if my life has no longer been my own, as if I have been infiltrated by an alien being who has taken over my mind. The quiet stillness that has veiled the house in comforting peace, has soothed my mind again, allowing it to think more clearly. At first, I had wondered where Alex disappeared to, but eventually the curiosity passed and instead now I revel in my new found freedom. I am beginning to carve out a new life again. I am beginning to feel safe.

It has become a habit of late to sit in the front living room in the evening, just as I used to do with mother. In readiness of the soap opera that is about to begin, I patter down the hallway to make a cup of cocoa, so that I can sip it while the latest drama unfolds. As I push open the kitchen door, on an evening just the same as every other evening, something in front of me makes me stop dead in my tracks. In the centre of the kitchen table is a mug of tea, sitting on top of an opaque glass placemat as if it has every business to be there. From my vantage point at the threshold of the room, I stare at the cup, whose tendrils of steam are wafting upwards towards the Artex ceiling and try to compute how it has come to be there. Tentatively, I divert my eyes from the table and allow them to search through the dimly lit room and into the far corner, where the light from the hallway does not reach.

Suddenly, a cold draught wafts towards me. Involuntarily I shiver as the chilly air reaches me. Automatically I pull my long blue knitted cardigan across my body more tightly, re-fastening the belt and squeezing it into my waist. Something about the action seems odd, even though it is one that I have performed many times. I cannot fathom what it is though and push the thought from my mind. For a more pressing thought has come to mind; the source of the cold air that I have not noticed before.

The room is rapidly becoming colder. Colourless vapour escapes from my mouth as the cool air mixes with my warm breath. I watch as it floats across the room and escapes through the open door, then melts away into the darkness outside, far beyond the reach of the light. My eyes follow the path of the vapour trail towards the bottom of the garden, bordered by dark green conifers that are usually encased in darkness and not visible from the house. Tonight though, something is different, something has changed. Above the regular pattern of the feather board fence, the dark outline of the trees is silhouetted against the navy-blue skyline, which is peppered with bright, silvery stars. The light cast from the crescent moon is shining onto the concrete path that bisects the garden. My eyes follow the path and are quickly drawn to the hunkering shadow that is in front of the trees in the far corner of the garden, which should be shrouded in darkness. But tonight it is not, for there is a light on in the shed. The shed that is always padlocked. The place I am not allowed to go.

My focus flicks back to the kitchen. Steeling myself against the scene I do not wish to unfold, I place my hand flat against the wall and fumble for the light switch. My heart is pounding as I summon up the courage to switch it on.

Light floods the room and I blink furiously against the sudden change. My eyes rest on the table in front of me as I gently allow them to become accustomed to the light. I cannot put it off any longer. Cautiously I raise my eyes then turn my head a little towards the door to the garden, which I can now see is half-open.

Immediately all my questions are answered by the presence of a figure that has appeared from the shadows and is now standing next to the half-glazed door, seemingly oblivious to the cold. The person is staring at me, dark eyes boring into the very depths of my soul, watching my every reaction. A grin slowly forms, accompanied by a glint of satisfaction in those dark eyes that displays the confidence that he is feeling, from the knowledge that I have now seen what he wants me to see. I wipe my clammy hands on the top of my trousers. The movement does not go unnoticed and the smile deepens, in acknowledgement of my discomfort.

'That's your tea,' the figure nods in the direction of the mug on the table.

Cautiously I reach out to pick it up, then pull my hand away again, unsure of whether or not I should drink it. A deep sigh comes from the far end of the room. Steeling myself against what could happen next, my fingers stretch out to take hold of the handle. Suddenly a shadow appears to the right of me and my hand is slapped out of the way, knocking the scalding liquid over onto the table in the process. I watch as the liquid spreads out across the table then drips down the table leg nearest to me, splashing onto my feet. At first, I do not feel the pain, even though the message that scalding liquid has landed onto the thin skin of my instep, takes only nanoseconds to be transported across the microscopic synapses to reach the cerebral cortex. Before my brain has even had the chance to interpret that message, my automatic reactions kick in and I remove my foot from the slipper to break its contact with the scalding wet material. I place my foot onto the cold vinyl floor to provide some relief from the searing sensation that my brain is now interpreting to be coming from the top of my left foot, even if it is just a simple distraction technique.

A sharp peal of laughter fills the room. 'What do you think you're doing? Put that back on, you'll get a cold foot,' the voice quietly commands.

'But it's wet,' I whisper, knowing that this is the wrong thing to say but that there is no alternative. My knees begin to tremble and a weakness spreads down my legs to such an extent that I do not know how they are keeping me upright.

A face suddenly looms in front of me, nose almost touching mine. 'How dare you talk to me like that. Who do you think you are?'

My wrist is gripped in such a vice-like manner, that it leaves me in no doubt that a red welt will appear by morning. Without warning I am being yanked across the room, bashing my thigh on the corner of the table with the force of the movement. Somehow a chair has ended up in the centre of the room, and a large hand swats it sharply out of the way. The sound of the chair legs scraping against the floor makes me wince - the vinyl flooring will be marked and this will be held against me.

Suddenly I am outside in the cold, dark garden,

being roughly pulled down the concrete steps and onto the path that leads to the shed. Through the small Perspex window, I can see an uncovered lightbulb burning brightly in the centre of the shed. The light casts an eerie yellow glow around the outer edge of the door and through the keyhole, where a long metal key is already in the lock, waiting to be turned. I cannot breathe, I do not know what is inside. I do not want to know.

I stare transfixed at the key as a large, calloused hand stiffly twists it in the padlock, which has rusted from the dampness that always seems to linger at the bottom of the garden. The conifer trees that line the perimeter look menacing in the moonlight, the soft breeze ruffles the coarse dark green fronds, creating a sinister whisper that makes me shiver. I am reminded of the sound of waves breaking on the beach on my childhood holidays and for a moment I am transported back there, sitting on the beach, the warmth of the sand burning the underside of my bare legs, feeling the sharp grains running through my fingers as I search for tiny shells. Then I am transported to another memory as the aroma from the decaying leaves gathered at the base of the thick trunk, remind me of the pungent salty seaweed that peppered the slippery black rocks at the place where my brother died. The comforting mirage of the beach where I once felt happy dissipates again and the soft vision melts away into a darkness that I fear to go.

The sharp click of a lock being sprung brings me back to the present again. I open my eyes to see a hand reaching forward to remove the padlock, then the bolt is slid across the vertical wooden slats. I cannot move. My feet are frozen to the concrete path below.

'You do know that this is for your own good, don't

you?'

I nod, knowing that it is what is expected of me. I am rewarded by a hand motioning for me to enter into the small space. The faint aroma of wood preservative evokes memories of my father standing at the back of the shed, tinkering with radios and repairing clocks to earn a little extra money so that we could afford luxuries like a week at a caravan park on the coast. Involuntarily, I smile at the memory of him picking up a clock from the work bench, proudly showing me what he had been working on that day.

The vision shatters into a thousand pieces that splinter into the abyss, as a thick arm snakes around my waist to pull the wooden door behind me shut with a loud click that cuts into the stillness. Above the heady aroma of damp wood, I catch a waft of aftershave that I do not recognise. Fleetingly I wonder what it is, knowing that it will be forever ingrained in my memory. Suddenly I notice a rope being picked up from the rough wooden floor. I watch out of the far corner of my visual field as the rope is wound tightly around the hand that only moments ago was around my waist.

'Turn around.'

My heart thuds so forcefully that my head begins to swim. A dark shadow fills my vision, then clears again. My feet feel as if they are encased in lead. I do not seem to be able to move them from the spot where I am standing, still at the entrance of the shed. My legs tremble and almost give way completely as a sudden weakness shoots through them. I am certain that pleasure will be felt at the sight of my discomfort, so I quickly try to regain control over the involuntary actions of my body.

Then my world is plunged into a thick blackness as a heavy cloth is pulled over my head, the rough material scraping over the bridge of my slender nose. I cannot breathe. I must focus on my breath, inhale, exhale, breathe in, breathe out, just keep breathing. Perhaps it would be better if I did pass out, or even suffocate, then at least I would be afforded the luxury of ignorance of what is about to come.

There is movement towards the back of the shed, heavy shoes pressing down on floorboards, which softly groan under the weight. The movement stops, then in the silence that follows, I hear another noise. Something is picked up then set down again to one side with a dull clank, as if tools are being moved from one place to another. It sounds as if someone is looking for something.

'Ah here it is,' the voice says quietly from within the darkness.

I scarcely hear the heavy footsteps approach over the rushing noise in my inner ears from my racing heart, the beat pulsating through me as if to protect me from hearing anymore. Bile splashes up into the top of my oesophagus and into my mouth, accompanied by a wave of nausea, which I fight to suppress, leaving me with a bitter taste in my mouth. Then I hear it, a metallic thump, followed by a sharp click, a sound so vivid that it cuts through my fear in an instance. I do not want to listen, but can do nothing else. I cannot block out the sound of a plug being forced into a socket and being switched on, nor the prevailing silence, which heralds a pause in the proceedings, as if waiting for the final curtain to fall before the applause. For a moment there is silence, then suddenly the shed is filled with the thunderous gnawing sound of a chainsaw.

CHAPTER FOURTEEN

It is early morning. The day is beginning to break over the line of poplar trees at the far end of the park. A thin golden line has appeared over the horizon and is now pushing back the gradually receding darkness. The emerging light casts elongated shadows across the lush green lawn, morphing the nine-foot-high trees into sinister sentries, who are protectively surveying their dominion below. A gentle breeze caresses the shrubbery nearest to the Victorian wrought-iron gate, which is closed but not locked, as if a ghostly hound is ferreting about underneath the coarse branches, searching to discover the source of the scent that it is following. To the right of the gate, close to the metal perimeter fence, the dim yellow light from a nearby streetlamp reveals a shadow lying motionless inside the ornate Victorian shelter, which is pushed back behind the path amongst the overgrown shrubs. The empty bottle lying askew beneath the slatted bench, informs me that the occupant of the shelter has fallen into a drunken stupor and is of no immediate danger to my plans.

I know that I will not have long to wait. She is a creature of habit, walking the small brown dog at the same time every morning, just after the sun has begun to rise. It is my favourite time of the day - that moment before the world has fully awoken, when there is a peaceful energy that cannot be felt at any other time. A quiet hope for what the day may bring.

It is also her favourite time of the day. I can tell this by the way she is skipping along the footpath. The little dog, who is trotting faithfully at her heels, periodically looks up at the girl for reassurance. The vivid red of the dog's leash and thick winter coat tells me that the animal is well loved by its owner, who is wearing a matching woollen coat, firmly fastened around her slender waist. She holds tightly onto the leash that is wound around her right hand, which is protected from the bite of the morning chill by a thin grey glove. Her other hand reaches up to tuck a loose tendril of hair back up into an over-sized woollen baker's cap, which is pulled down tightly over her ears, to keep out the damp mist that is curling around the warmth of a nearby streetlamp.

There is no one else walking the streets, only the occasional car passing through to take its weary occupant's home after a long night at work or perhaps they are awake early to take over the next shift. Perhaps they have even come from the enormous red-brick factory that dwarfs the end of the road; an imposing Victorian building that is safely contained from the remainder of society by vast iron gates that have somehow survived the war effort. From my current vantage point, I cannot see the stately gates, but I recall their existence from my previous visits to the area.

The sun is now rising further up into the sky, leaving streaks of pink and purple in its wake, cutting across the impenetrable darkness, which is beginning to recede and concede to the light of day. The girl reaches the outside of the park, unhooks the latch and pushes the metal gate open across the pathway, the rusted hinges noisily protest at the movement.

The sound cuts though the silence, and for a moment I fear that someone in the line of houses opposite must surely have heard it, but no, the street remains as peaceful as it was only moments ago.

It is nearly time. I watch as the girl passes through the opening left by the gate that is now at right angles to the perimeter fence. She strides confidently up the path with the dog following closely behind. Momentarily, she pauses to allow the hound to sniff about underneath a large Hebe, then she unclips the leash and continues along the centre of the path until she is swallowed up by the blackness, far out of reach of the comforting light of the streetlamps that line the road around the edge of the recreational area. I fight to quell my anxiety as the girl disappears from view. I know from previous occasions that the path she will have taken, curls around the perimeter of the park, where it is partially hidden by trees and overgrown shrubs that have been forgotten in this quiet suburb. This is where I will meet her.

My attention is drawn back to the entrance that the girl has just passed through. A large rectangular sign to the right of the entrance adorns a simplistic map, showing the official walking route through the park. Even from this distance, the name 'Allenby Park' is visible in large white letters. I am unable to decipher the text beneath the map, but surmise that it will provide anyone who is interested with some context and history to the park along with the name it has been given. My eyes wander across the road to the top of the street, close to the old red-brick factory. A white metal street sign fixed at the corner of the brick wall, tells me that my car is currently parked in 'Allenby Road'. Perhaps the name of the factory owner was also 'Allenby', and it was he who had built the row of terraced houses for loyal employees, so that they could enjoy a more decent standard of living than most of the working class of that era would have endured. I wonder what the factory would have been making at the time when the houses had first been built and whether or not the conditions inside would have afforded the men, women and children who worked there, a greater degree of safety than the other factories of the Victorian period. It is likely that working conditions inside the enormous building were far more dangerous than the impression given by the owners' flamboyant benevolence in providing its workers with nearby accommodation and even more generously, a small stamp of grass that was later defined as a 'park'. Ironically, the factory's only recent infamy was from a picket line that had blocked the entrance to the factory one week late last summer, to protest against inequality of wages for the women and the Albanian immigrants who worked on the shop floor; a far cry from the ideal notion of a public image that the Allenby's had wanted to purvey through their façade of generosity.

Stealthily I open the car door, then push it gently shut with a click that seems loud given the stillness of the hour. Although the streets are still empty, a degree of paranoia washes over me as I open the boot to retrieve the bag that I keep in there for such occasions. I resist the urge to look around me. If someone is watching from a bedroom window, I would be drawing attention to myself, and of course this is something I wish to avoid at all costs.

Plunging my hand deep inside the bag, I retrieve a length of sturdy rope, which I coil around my left hand out of habit, followed by a rag that has been kept for many years in the boot of the car in case of emergencies. Lastly, I retrieve my favourite hunting knife, with its serrated edge and razor-sharp tip that I sharpened yesterday. Carefully I secrete the knife up the sleeve of my dark grey duffle coat, with its matching hood and light brown toggles that serve to fasten the item instead of a zip. The coldness of the metal against my warm skin is a comforting reminder for me that so far everything is going to plan. Even the sharp tip that is biting into my forearm is not unwelcome, for it reassures me that I have prepared well for the task ahead.

A subtle glance around the surrounding streets, reaffirms that I am still alone. I am ready to proceed. I push the boot lid down gently until it clicks, then step up onto the kerb to walk the few yards to the same metal gates the girl passed through a few short moments ago. The streetlamps, which are still lit even though dawn is fast approaching, cast shadows across the path, the artificial light creating all manner of strange shapes that flicker and move, like ghosts dancing in the moonlight. I wonder how the girl is not fearful of coming to such a place on her own. Perhaps her youth affords her the arrogant ignorance that nothing untoward could possibly ever happen to her, or perhaps she feels safer out here on her own in the darkness then she does in her own home, a sentiment that I understand well.

As I begin to walk along the path in the direction the girl took earlier, I almost feel a pang of regret that in a few moments the girl's innocence will be destroyed forever and the world that she trusts and believes in, will be turned upside down. But as quickly as it has come, these foolish thoughts are quashed again. There is no room for sentiment, there is much work that still needs to be done, there are many lessons that still need to be taught.

Halfway along the first stretch of the path, a little way past the shelter and its still sleeping occupant, I pause for a moment to listen to the sound of the wind swishing through the leaves of a nearby sycamore tree. It seems as if it is whispering to me and I wonder what it is saying, if it is telling me to go on or to go back. For it is not just the girl's life that will be changed forever in the next few moments, but mine also, as I make one more step towards the restitution I have desired for so long. I cannot turn back now, I have done so much work to get to this point, I must press on.

Quietly I move forward, taking care not to walk at too fast a pace in case I catch up with her too quickly. I do not want to risk being seen until the last possible moment. My eyes are fixed to the ground to avoid stepping on any twigs that may be lying littered around and could alert the dog to my presence. I am grateful for the emerging daylight that is lighting my path sufficiently well that I can avoid tripping on the mushy detritus below - for I have now reached the point where the light from the nearby streetlamps is unable to penetrate though the thick shrubbery that lines the perimeter fence.

I pass through the stillness, with only the rustling of the leaves from the overhanging trees whose roots are encroaching the concrete path, for company. Surely by now I should have seen the girl? Perhaps I have mis-calculated the route or misjudged her pace? A shock of fear strikes through me and nausea rises up from my stomach at the sudden thought that perhaps the girl has gone. It is conceivable that there is another gate on the other side of the park hidden by the foliage, that I may have missed when I walked around the perimeter three days ago. I hope that I am wrong.

All of a sudden, she is there, a slight figure, partially veiled by an overgrown Hebe that has entirely taken over one side of the path. The girl has stopped several feet in front of me, her beautiful face which is lit up by the soft light is even more beguiling than the other times I have seen her. I take a deep breath and relax a little, my plans have not been thwarted. The time has come.

Distracted by the angelic vision before me, I have momentarily forgotten the dog, who is now running up the path towards me, tail wagging as it yelps with excitement at finding another living creature. Quickly I shrink back into a nearby rhododendron bush and wait for the girl to appear as she must surely do. Of course, I am right, I have watched her for too long not to know how she would react. The girl moves quickly up the path towards the dog. She scoops it up into the crook of her arm as if holding a petulant toddler who is having a tantrum. She nuzzles her face into the dog's coarse hair, whilst chastising him ineffectually for his momentary disappearance, just as a mother would do with a child who has wandered off out of sight in a shop in the briefest of moments when she has turned her back on them to reach into her bag for her purse to pay for the groceries.

I wait until she is passes me, then slink silently out onto the path behind her. The dog stares at me wide eyed, from his position in his owner's arms, as I move closer. Then suddenly the moment I have been anticipating is upon us. She is mine.

CHAPTER FIFTEEN

I know that I am awake, even though I cannot see. The blindfold is bound so tightly around my eyes that not even the tiniest chink of light can filter through the thick material. It is quiet. Too quiet. I want to listen out for the noises that will tell me if I am alone or not, but I am too afraid to, in case the sliver of hope I feel in the pit of my stomach is washed away again by the tears that will surely come if I hear sounds that I do not wish to hear. I imagine there is someone sitting cross-legged at the back of the shed, slumped deep inside the bowed material of the old striped deck chair, which is normally folded up underneath the work bench. In my mind they are watching, silently, waiting for me to summon up the courage to try to escape and when I do, I will be punished again and this time I might not survive. The image will not leave my head and leaves my limbs so weak with fear, that I cannot move.

Somewhere towards the top of the enormous conifer that dominates the bottom of the garden, I hear the faint chirping of a blackbird, who is heralding the beginning of the day. I listen, enthralled, allowing the small feeling of hope to grow stronger as the blackbird's voice grows louder and more joyous with every passing moment. It is only when the singing pauses, allowing silence to momentarily descend, that

I realise there is one sound that is missing from the cacophony; there are no sounds of breathing. I am alone. I sit still and listen carefully, to be certain that I am not mistaken, but I am not. There is no one else in the shed.

My arms are stiff from being held at the same angle that they were forced into the previous night. Tentatively, I wiggle my fingers a little at a time, trying to ignore the stabbing pains that are shooting across my hands and up my wrists, as the blood begins to circulate again. The pain makes me nauseous so I stop for a moment, afraid that I will vomit into the rough hessian bag that is still wrapped tightly around my head. As time passes, the pain begins to ebb away into a dull throb and so I begin the arduous task again.

During the next few minutes, I stop and start the painful process over and over again, until at last I have enough feeling back in my fingers to begin the torturous task of picking at the threads of the rope that is fastened around my wrists. I try not to think about what would have happened if my wrists had been bound behind my back.

As time passes, I become aware of the basic needs of the human body; food, water and elimination of waste. My mouth has dried up from breathing through the material over my face and I can barely move my cracked lips, nor swallow the little saliva I am able to produce in my current state of dehydration. I begin to imagine the taste of a cool glass of water, the soft liquid swirling around my mouth, soothing and healing and for a few moments I stop working on the rope, consumed by the thought, the burning desire for something so fundamental that has been denied to me for so long. My stomach feels as if it has contracted from the gnawing acid that is eating away at the lining and bubbling up into the top of my oesophagus towards my mouth, as if a baby bird is awaiting a tasty morsel from its mother. Suddenly my attention is drawn away from the burning pain in my throat. My sense of smell, which has been heightened by my temporary loss of sight, detects a familiar odour that has just reached the olfactory cells in my nostrils. I am no longer in need of a toilet.

Frantically I begin to pick at the rope with greater determination, spurred on by my body's desperate need for water, until at last, I reach the last few threads. Testing to see if my work has yielded success, I pull my wrists apart, feeling the bindings give a little, noting the progress made from the same movement I performed a little earlier. This time though luck is on my side, with just a little more pressure, the rope disintegrates and falls onto the floorboards below with a satisfying thud. Automatically I rub each wrist in turn, encouraging the circulation to flow more freely. There is a burning sensation from where the rope has chafed against my soft skin and I know that it will be some days before the dull, throbbing pain subsides.

With my hands now freed, I remove the hood from my head. Even though dawn has only just broken and the sun has not yet risen fully overhead, my eyes blink painfully at the sudden influx of light. I shut them again, allowing the darkness to soothe them until the red blotches dancing across my closed lids disappear. Then I re-open them, much more slowly this time, waiting until the snowstorm swirling across my vision dissipates before opening them fully.

Once my vision has settled, I allow my eyes to comb through the shed, drinking in every part of it in turn, as if seeing it for the first time. The deckchair, which is still tucked away underneath my father's workbench, is covered in a thick layer of dust that has discoloured the white stripes and dulled those that were once a vibrant red. The tools that my father always laid out on the top of the bench are gone, along with the elongated khaki tool bag that has always been kept in the cupboard underneath the workbench, whose door is now hanging open. I remember when my father made that cupboard. It had taken him a whole weekend and he had been glad of it, as the task had kept him away from my mother. Equally, I had been glad of the opportunity to sit in the stripy deckchair and watch my father peacefully work. Suddenly an urge overwhelms me to touch the object that my father had revered so much. I stoop down and run my index finger along the top edge of the cupboard, recalling the effort he had put into planing and sanding it, until the doors were an even thickness and the edges were smooth enough to paint. Of course, mother was not pleased at the absence of her husband for the second weekend that was needed to complete the painting of the cupboard and the argument that followed, tarnished the pleasure my father had found in his work to such an extent, that he never again made another piece of furniture.

I try to push the cupboard door shut, but it has warped in the damp atmosphere of the uninsulated shed to such an extent that it no longer fits flush onto the frame and the marrying parts of the lock that my father fitted no longer marry together.

A sudden wave of dizziness washes over me, a reminder that I have not eaten since yesterday. I rest my hand upon the wooden bench to steady myself and stay there until the dizziness passes. The moment passes and I test out my newly found resolve, by daring myself to look up along the flat wooden surface to the far side of the bench, where my father's tools should be laid out neatly, equidistant from each other. At the far end, an object that does not belong in my father's shed, catches my attention. The sight of it makes me heave so violently that I double over and cannot prevent myself from vomiting onto my feet, droplets of yellowy chyme splashing onto the wooden floor below. I close my eyes, but the image is still there in my mind, along with the memory of the sharp, metallic sound of a chainsaw resonating through a quiet space - switched on and ready to use.

I struggle to quell the rising panic. My heart flutters so rapidly, that I fear it will burst inside my rib cage. My breath quickens, short shallow breaths that leave me in danger of passing out from the reduced levels of oxygen now pumping to my brain. Somewhere in the back of my mind, a memory is sparked of a television programme I once watched with my mother about the history of British asylums and how many of the women incarcerated there were suffering from emotional trauma rather than a malignant mental illness. I recall one woman who had regularly hyperventilated to make herself faint, which at first had puzzled the doctors, who could find no physical cause for it. Eventually it was decided that it was caused by an imbalance of the brain and the poor woman, whose aim had been to avoid an arranged marriage to someone she despised, had instead led to her being lobotomised and spending the rest of her days locked in an institution. The story has since remained ingrained in my memory and I vividly recall the techniques reported in the programme, that could be used to gain control over anxiety. By the time the memory of the documentary has faded away again, I have repeated the techniques several times over, and my pulse rate has once again settled to a normal resting rhythm. I re-open my eyes and the memory from the previous night dissipates. I am back alone in the shed again, with only the birdsong outside to keep me company.

My ankles are tied together with a much thicker rope than the one that bound my wrists. Slowly I move forwards, half shuffling, half jumping, inching myself closer and closer towards the centre of the workbench. I try to block out the dull throbbing sensation at the top of my legs. I know what he has done, but I cannot allow myself to think about that now. I need to concentrate on one thing at a time and right now I need to find a way to free myself. Fleetingly I wonder if he intended to leave me here to die. Somehow, I feel certain that he will not return.

I turn my attention towards finding something sharp enough to cut through the rope. There, on the top of the work bench, my father's' bow saw still hangs on a peg above the bench that he made and diligently installed over forty years ago. The scent of cleaning fluids and oil evokes memories of him standing right there, in front of where I am now. I can see him so clearly in my mind, his deeply lined forehead furrowed in concentration as he explained to me how to use the saw.

I pick up the bow saw and look it over. There, right at the bottom, just how I remembered it, is the pointed end that I cut myself on many years ago, when I helped father to cut up lengths of wood for making into a small table for the front sitting room. It has been a long time since the saw has been cared for and a deep covering of dust covers the handle. A deep, orange rust is beginning to form along the edges of the blade. Without thinking, I run my index finger across the tip of the blade and watch as a thin line of red appears across the soft pad, then pools into the creases of my fingerprint. It is still sharp.

My weary fingers protest as I defiantly grab hold of the orange handle of the saw, my wrists burn as I struggle to hold the blade in place above the centre point of the rope between my ankles. But I must ignore the pain and press on.

It takes all the courage I can muster to make the first cut. I am almost tempted to close my eyes, terrified that my hands might slip and instead of sawing through the thick rope, I will cut through my ankle bone. I take a few deep breaths to try to steady my shaking hands, then plunge the blade onto the top of the rope. The blade makes contact with the fibres and I release the breath that I did not realise I have been holding.

Progress is slow and painful. Every movement the blade makes sends shocking vibrations through exhausted bones, that are already sore from being tied up for so long. But with every slow second that passes, a shard of hope brightens within me that perhaps I might still walk out of this shed alive. Biting back the tears that have formed at the thought that I could soon be free, I try to concentrate instead on the monotony of the actions, cutting through the deep layers of rope, fibre by tiny fibre.

My confidence grows as the fibres melt away onto the floor below, but still, I dare not quite allow myself to feel hope that this will work; for hope, I have learnt, can be a cruel trick, and is something that I have not allowed myself to feel for very a long time.

I am almost there, only a few more strands of rope fibre left to cut through. My heart thumps hard, adrenaline pumping through the arteries to my brain and once more I reluctantly stop to allow my laboured breath to settle. As I rest, my attention is drawn away from the rope to the outside world, which has been long forgotten in this vacuous realm where my only focus has been on freeing myself. With nervous trepidation, I allow my consciousness to listen for sounds outside of the shed. Something is different, something has changed. For a moment, my mind that has been dulled by shock, cannot comprehend the change. Then I realise what it is - the birds have finished their dawn chorus. The stillness frightens me. I imagine that I can hear footsteps clipping up the concrete path; immaculately polished shoes that keep to the concrete path to avoid muddying them. I am not imagining it. I can hear footsteps.

Nausea rises up into the top of my dry throat, the sharp acids make me cough. I splutter as I try to suppress the automated response, fearful of being heard by whomever is outside. Without thinking, I throw the saw onto the back of the bench where it lands askew, shuddering and clattering onto the smooth wooden surface. I watch transfixed, as the movements gradually lessen, then stop completely. Realising the foolishness of my actions, I shut my eyes tightly and clasp my hands over my ears to shut out the world and whatever it is that is still moving up the path towards the shed. I do not want to hear it. I do not want to be here when that shed door opens.

Seconds feel like hours, as I hold my breath in anticipation, but the door does not open. The footsteps I have tried so desperately to block out, stop before they reach the bottom of the garden. There is a sharp clink as a metal dustbin lid is pulled up, followed by the thud of a bag being dropped into the void. The reassuring clank of the lid being replaced, tells me that the footsteps must belong to my neighbour.

As I let go of the breath that I have been holding, it rushes out of me in a huge whoosh of relief, which would be audible to anyone close enough to the shed, but the neighbour must have moved far enough away again, for the retreating footsteps are quickly followed by a door slamming shut. The realisation that I am not alone in this world, prods me out of the numbed stupor that I have retreated into. Even though the opportunity to ask for help is gone, the thought that there is another human being close by gives me the courage that I need to carry on.

I lean across the bench to reach out for the saw, which I hastily discarded only moments ago. Stretching out my right arm as far as it will reach, my fingertips brush across the tip of the blade. All of the feelings of frustration, fear and hopelessness that I have managed to somehow suppress up to this point, wash over me in a torrent that I cannot control. I slump to the floor as if in slow motion, collapsing onto the damp wooden floorboards, my right shoulder leaning against a vertical strut supporting the work bench, is all that keeps me upright. With my head bowed into my hands, I sob so vehemently that it feels as if it will never cease. I tell myself over and over that I am so close, I cannot give up now. I am so near to being free.

Eventually the emotions pass and I pull myself up into a standing position. I inhale deeply then release the breath slowly again. I do this several more times until I feel calm again, ready to face the challenge before me. Straightening my spine, I can feel the soreness of my bruised ribs as my torso pushes outwards and upwards. Just as I have seen on the yoga class on tv, I thrust my arms straight up into the air, then bend at the waist, pressing my tender stomach into the hard wooden bench as I lean forward over the bench. This time my fingers brush against the handle of the saw. I move it millimetre by millimetre towards me until at last my fingers are able to grasp hold of the blade.

My hands tighten around the saw, as an infant would do with a rattle, refusing to let go of it again. Ignoring the sharp pain as the blade bites into the soft flesh of my palms, I transfer my hold to the plastic handle then place the blade back onto the rope, where I begin to sever through the remaining fibres. At last, the rope falls away, softly falling onto the floorboards like a withered appendage. I throw the saw down onto the bench with a clatter, this time not caring how loud the sound is, then collapse, exhausted onto the floorboards.

A calm stillness shrouds the shed, as if the tense atmosphere of fear and uncertainty never existed; as if all that I experienced over the last twelve hours never occurred. Only the dull throbbing pain between my legs reminds me of the ordeal I have survived. I push the thought aside. It is not time yet to think of that.

My attention is once more drawn to the outside world. In the distance, a back door is slammed shut, followed by a dog barking as it catches the scent of the neighbourhood fox who often visits during the night to forage around the bins for some tasty morsel to eat. The world is awakening and here I am, still in this shed. Suddenly the desire to leave it and breathe in fresh air again becomes overwhelming. Instantly I forget my weariness, the pain from my bruised body and the fear that has not yet fully subsided. For a brief moment, I feel a mixture of relief and pride in all that I have achieved, but this elation quickly evaporates as the tight knot in the pit of my churning stomach returns. It is time to leave this place, the place where I now feel safe in the certainty that I am alone. I must leave.

CHAPTER SIXTEEN

This one is different from the others; I can tell already. She is lying quietly in the footwell in the back of the car, her ankles and wrists bound with the rope that I usually keep in the boot, neatly coiled up like a snake awaiting its prey. The silence is unnerving me for this did not happen with the others. I cannot decide if she is submissively accepting her fate or if she is cunningly trying to lull me into a false sense of security whilst she plots her escape. A small part of me wishes to believe that perhaps she is the right one for me, the one who will be able to stay forever as my companion, who will love me unconditionally, respect me and want to care for me. But in the back of my mind there is a small voice niggling at me, telling me that I should not trust her. She could be playing games, biding her time to trick me. All my hard work will be lost if she escapes.

It does not take long to reach the Walton estate. I make a right turn into Cornwall Road then pull sharply over onto the side of the road, as close as possible to the entrance of the passageway that separates the back yards of the houses on Ivry Street from those on Chester Road. The dark passageway is peppered at regular intervals with makeshift wooden gates that allow the occupants to drag their rubbish bins out from their backyards and through the passageway to the nearest kerb, where they dutifully stand on sentry for collection every fortnight. The bins are always overflowing; putrid rubbish riddled with maggots in the summer months; frozen solid with a crisp layer of frost in the winter. It is a wonder that the passageway is not littered more given the reduction of collections due to a shortage of refuse lorry drivers. Perhaps I have misjudged the level of integrity of the occupants in this part of town and they care more for their environment than I first gave them credit for, though I think it unlikely given that I was once one of them.

Dawn is breaking, bathing the roof tops of the houses on the opposite side of Cornwall Road in a warm light. Behind me, a cold darkness still encompasses the side of the road containing 6 Ivry Street, which seems fitting given what lies within its red brick walls. It is as if the universe knows of the secrets held within. I wonder for how long they can be contained.

The streets are still quiet. In the distance, there is a low whining tone from a milk float that is travelling up and down each of the roads in turn to deliver milk, butter and eggs to whomever has enough money to pay off the weekly bill without going into arrears. The sound of the milk float evokes a long forgotten memory of one occasion when I was staying at grandfather's house, and was awoken at 5am by the unfamiliar clinking sound of a glass bottle being roughly placed onto the doorstep below my bedroom window, rapidly followed by the front door being opened and a gruff voice with a thick Irish accent asking, 'Why in god's name are you leaving a bottle of milk at my front door?'

From my vantage point behind the net curtain, safely hidden away from the wrath of my grandfather, I could hear the milkman stammer in a thin, apologetic voice, 'An order was placed with the Co-op shop in Margaret Street last week.'

'That can't be right,' grandfather had spluttered. I could so easily visualise droplets of spittle landing onto the poor unsuspecting milkman, who was no doubt by now shrinking away from the irate ogre, his rounded jowls reddened in anger, his large frame filling the doorway in the intimidating manner that I witnessed on numerous occasions.

Feeling a little bit braver, I had decided to risk peering through the yellowing net curtain, which was stretched tightly across the dirty bedroom window, in the hope of seeing the scene unfolding below. I had craned my neck downwards, my nose and left cheek pressed up against the cold glass, which was covered in a thin layer of frost that had formed on the inside of the pane. Below the window, clouds of transparent vapour billowed out into the street from the doorway, where they dissipated as soon as they reached the warmth of the yellow streetlamp. The fog disappeared, to reveal the shadowy figure of my grandfather, his thick torso leaning against the white doorframe with its flaking woodwork. His right foot was firmly wedged between the door and the frame, preventing it from closing and inadvertently locking him out of the house. In his left hand, a roll-up was burning, the trail of smoke from it mingling with the vapour being exhaled with great force, from the visibly irritated occupant of number 6 Ivry Street.

Grandfather was wearing a white vest, tinged greyed with age and a pair of faded beige trousers, top button unfastened, zip undone halfway. His attire told me that he had spent the night sitting bolt upright in the faded wingback chair located at the back of the front living room, with a glass of whisky still clutched tightly in one hand. How that glass never fell from his clasp whilst he was passed out in a drunken stupor, I do not know. In all the times that I had stayed in that house, I never once witnessed it fall onto the raspberry swirled carpet that had been laid across the whole of the downstairs of the house by grandfather's nephew, who was a jack-of-all trades builder. I firmly believed that the reason why the glass never fell from his grasp, was because not even an inanimate object would have dared to disobey my grandfather.

I had fought back the almost overwhelming urge to run downstairs, displace the foot encased in a tartan slipper that was wedging the door open and slam shut the front door, leaving grandfather, half-clothed on the streets. I could imagine the punishment that I would have to endure for such an action, but chose not to bring such images to mind and instead released the fantasy I had created of even the smallest semblance of revenge that I could muster.

'I..I..I..I.. just deliver the milk, I don't have anything to do with taking the orders,' the milkman stuttered. The weak light cast from the streetlamp on the opposite side of the road, revealed the man's face to be as white as the bottle of milk he was holding. The tension was almost unbearable, as I pressed my cheek up against the windowpane, trying to see how grandfather would react.

Grandfather snorted loudly. 'Then I'll be visiting the shop as soon as it opens and I won't be paying for your mistake neither,' he said, grabbing the bottle from the unsuspecting milkman.

The milkman swiftly backed up, tripping over his own feet as he traversed across the pavement and down onto the tarmac road, where his float was perched, engine still running. I pulled back a little from the window and watched as he scrambled into the vehicle, almost tripping over the trouser hem of the navy-blue uniform issued by the dairy, which had become unravelled and was dangling ominously. The vehicle pulled out into the road, its familiar engine whirring as it quickly sped off into the darkness, bottles clinking against metal bottle holders in the back of the low, open vehicle.

As grandfather turned to shut the front door again, he noticed a small figure watching from the tiny bedroom window. He jabbed the cigarette, which was by now almost down to a stub, into his alcohol-fumed mouth, then placed his hands onto his hips and stared at the child, as if it were his fault that the milk had been delivered. The child was familiar with that particular look, and knew that he would be punished for witnessing the scene, but not as much of a punishment as grandmother would be given when it was discovered it was she, who had placed the milk order. I understood her reasoning for undertaking such a risk; to avoid being punished if the milk at the breakfast table was not as fresh as grandfather would have liked, but I also knew that this explanation would never reach my grandfather, not just because he would not listen, but because he would just find another way to torture her and that could be far worse than what she had already endured. It was the only time that I had closed my eyes and silently prayed to any higher being that might exist, that grandmother would not reveal who had been standing next to her in the Co-op as she placed the order. I did not do it again, for my prayers were left unanswered.

The memory of my grandparents fades into the night sky, melting away as the morning light beings to strengthen, pushing back the images of my past into the dark abyss again. I turn my attention back to the task that has become my life's focus, the destiny I am compelled to fulfil before I move on to the next world. I *twist around to look at the girl, who is lying motionless in the footwell. A flicker of fear shoots through me that perhaps something catastrophic has occurred and she has already died. But then the index finger on her left hand twitches and a torrent of relief floods through me. She is still alive.*

I reach my left hand down into the darkness and unclip my seatbelt, pulling it across me so that it could retract automatically into the holder. Quietly I open the door and peek my head out through the small gap, checking the road both ahead and behind for anyone who might be out for an early morning dog walk, or on their way to work for the next shift. Confident there is no one nearby, I push the door open a little wider and step out of the car, my shoes landing softly onto the tarmac, whose thin layer of morning frost sparkles in the light of the moon.

There is a bitter chill in the air. I pull my woolen coat around me tightly and re-wrap the grey checked scarf around my neck more closely. Gently I push the car door shut, noting the familiar soft click of the mechanism inside, then walk around the car bonnet with its faded paintwork. In the centre of the bumper is a large dent caused by a minor collision with a lamppost. The previous owner allegedly had a fondness for gin and did not consider that driving a vehicle should deter him from partaking in his favourite pastime.

Stepping over the gulley, which is littered with the usual debris found in urban environments; discarded cigarette ends, cans of cheap lager and chocolate wrappers, I move up onto the pavement. Another glance up and down the street tells me that I am still alone - apart from the girl lying prone in the rear footwell of my car of course. I reach out and clasp hold of the handle of the rear passenger door and immediately regret my decision not to wear gloves, as the coldness of the steel bites into the underside of my fingers.

A whooshing sound nearby startles me. Automatically I release my hand, allowing it to drop to my side and slink backwards until I am close to the red brick wall, which comprises the last house in Ivry Street. From out of the light mist that is swirling around the lamppost at the far end of Cage Lane, a shadow appears. A paper boy races towards me on a shiny red bike that he was no doubt given on his last birthday. I expect that the boy comes from the other side of Seaton Road, where the parents are affluent enough to buy a brand new bike for their child's birthday, rather than being forced to wrap up a battered hand me down in plain brown paper, typical of the children who reside in the streets where I am now standing.

I watch from the safety of the shadows as the boy pelts along the road, makes a sharp turn into Cornwall Road, then heads off towards the corner shop. At the speed he is travelling I could surmise that he is yet again late in collecting the early morning newspapers for delivery, but it is just as likely from the look of apparent joy on the boy's face, that he is just enjoying the simple pleasure of riding a most treasured bike as quickly as he dares, feeling the wind whipping through his thick dark blond hair, that should have been covered by the light blue helmet, with its lightning shaped white streak across the centre of both sides, dangling from the handlebars. The smirk on the boy's lips reveals the rebellious pleasure he is feeling in this precise moment at his blatant defiance of his well-meaning parents, who have a tendency to smother their only child for fear of losing him. I cannot imagine how it could feel to be loved in such a way, to have parents whose only waking thought was to nurture and protect their child. A pang of jealousy bites into the deepest part of my psyche. I will never know how that child feels.

The boy makes a right turn and is lost from view. The road is empty once more but still, I check both ends of the street to ensure there is no one else close by. Satisfied that the neighbourhood is quiet once again, I move out of the shadows and walk across the crisp asphalt path to the car. Once more my fingers make contact with the cold steel handle, but this time there are no further interruptions. My index finger pushes up the button hidden on the underside of the door, followed by a quiet clunk as the door mechanism is released. I pull open the door then take a step back, to allow it to swing open wide enough to allow me to crane my neck into the dark void.

I allow my eyes to adjust to the dimness then peer inside the cavernous interior. The girl is still lying in the same position in the footwell, her tiny frame almost covered by shadows. I do not know why I feel surprised by this, perhaps I envisaged that she has been plotting to escape and has somehow managed to free herself from her bonds. But of course, nothing has changed and I allow the thought to come into my mind that perhaps this is the one that I have been waiting for.

I reach in and grab her upper arm, pulling her into an upright seated position. She winces at the sudden movement and I pause to allow her stiff body to become accustomed to the new position. Slowly I exhale, controlling the breath into a steady flow as I wait patiently to see how she reacts to the change in circumstance. At every moment I am testing her and now we have reached the most critical time, where I will learn if the girl can be trusted, or if she will make an attempt to escape. Although her blindfold prevents her from seeing her surroundings, she will be able to hear the sounds from the neighbourhood that will tell her that there are people nearby; the low hum from the milk float that is gradually weaving its way through the identical narrow terraced streets; the tingly bell the paper boy rings before he hurtles around the corner, warning anyone who might be travelling unseen towards him from the opposite direction; the shrill call from the blackbird perched on the topmost branch of the cherry tree that stands on a small patch of grass at the end of the road, which serves as a recreation ground for the local children. A rope hangs from one of the lower branches of the gnarly tree, a short, thick plank of wood fixed across the bottom serves as a makeshift seat for the swing. One side of the rope trails hopelessly onto the grass, a reflection of the lost souls who merely exist in this desolate place, their childhood dreams shattered by the constrictions imposed by a class-based society.

She does nothing. She sits still in the same position I placed her in, not moving or uttering a sound. I decide to reward her good behaviour by unpicking the ropes that are bound around her ankles, so that she can step out of the car more easily. Her knees have become stiff from lying in the same position for so long and she moves awkwardly. I watch as she reaches out to clutch onto the doorframe, forgetting that her wrists are still bound. The girl stumbles and I lean forward to catch her slight frame just in time to prevent her from falling, but not enough to prevent her from hitting her forehead on the top of the door. She winces loudly, then regains her composure.

Roughly I grab hold of her upper arm and guide her across the gap between the car and the pavement. The road is still quiet but another glance along

Cornwall Road reveals the presence of a light in the front bedroom of the house nearest to the entrance to the passageway, that had not been there earlier. The sun is beginning to rise more quickly, its weak morning rays shine through the branches of the cherry tree at the end of the road, leaving strange shadows dancing along the road towards us. We must move more quickly.

I guide the girl out of the car and up onto the pavement, then pause for a moment to quietly push the door shut again, hearing the reassuring click when the process is complete. Another light has now appeared, this time in the hallway of the house directly opposite where the car is parked. I cup my hand around the girl's elbow and push her towards the entrance to the passageway, which is still encased in thick blackness. Forgetting that she cannot see, I pull her into the void, her left leg narrowly misses a rubbish bin that is jutting out onto the cobbled path, her right knee scrapes across the corner of the brick wall running along the side of the path. In the dim light, I see a shadowy figure reach down, automatically reaching out to rub the injured knee, my arm, which is still holding onto her elbow almost loses grip with the suddenness of the movement. I stumble and my left foot makes contact with a discarded bottle, which clatters loudly against the cobbles. A light switches on in the rear downstairs room of No 4 Ivry Street and the back door swiftly opens.

''ello, is anyone there?' a gruff voice says from behind the five foot high gate.

Realising my mistake, I remove the blindfold. The girl looks at me, the whites of her eyes shining brightly against the dimness of the alleyway. I can see that she is trying to decide what to do. Should she call out for help, or would that be too much of a risk to take given that she does not know how I would react? She hesitates, just a little too long and the moment is lost. The figure behind the gate shuffles back into the safety of his kitchen and shuts the door again, locking it behind him.

We stand motionless in the centre of the path until the kitchen light is disappears again and is replaced by the ceiling light on the upstairs landing. The bathroom light is switched on and even from this distance, the sound of water running through the drainpipes is audible. A shadow appears on the other side of the bathroom blind, where the man is washing away the previous night's slumber.

The pause in our journey provides opportunity to survey the alleyway in which we are standing. The sides of the path are littered with foot high weeds and discarded household items; cardboard boxes, empty cans of cheap lager and even an old mop, its head so worn with use that it has been rendered almost bald. We stand side by side, surveying our surroundings, absorbing every detail and storing it in our minds.

When I am certain that the danger has passed, I weave the girl around the debris until we reach the gate of No 6. It is not locked - the number of times the gate has been kicked open left me with the conclusion that it is easier just to leave it unlocked. The gamble has paid off, as the gate has been left undamaged ever since. And in any case, there is little in the house for anyone to steal and I am certain that the local thieves are fully aware of this.

Gently I lift the metal latch and push open the gate, wincing at the sound, ever conscious of the speed and intensity that sound travels through the stillness of the night. The bottom of the gate has swollen and dropped on one side, it scrapes across the cobbles before coming to a halt, leaving a gap just wide enough for an adult to squeeze through. I lead the girl through the opening and onto the cobbles, which have been worn down over the years by the previous occupants of the house, leaving a shallow groove of a pathway to the back door. The girl tentatively steps across the yard, taking care not to slip on the light dusting of frost that has not yet dissipated with the warmth of the rising sun. I reach behind her and quietly close the gate again, but this time I fix a padlock onto the bolt that transects the inside of the wooden frame. We do not wish to be disturbed.

CHAPTER SEVENTEEN

I do not know how I have come to be back in the house. Nor do I remember walking upstairs, but somehow I must have managed to, for I am now sitting in a steaming bath, using up a whole weekly allowance of water and instead of the usual tepid liquid, the water is so hot that my skin has turned a bright salmon pink. The floor next to the bath is littered with the empty bottles of every container in the bathroom that were once filled with bubble bath and shower gel. The concoction of lavender and vanilla produces an odd mix of fragrances, but even so, it cannot rid me of the stench of damp walls, urine and fear, that is still ingrained on my senses. Nor can I relax, despite the seductive efforts of the soothing atmosphere, for I cannot hide the truth from myself; I do not know where he has gone to and until I do, I am not safe.

I lie in the bath for over an hour until the water is almost cold. Reluctantly I pull myself up, clutching tightly onto the side of the bath to steady myself as I step out over the edge of the bath, placing one foot after another onto the cream bathmat. I cannot yet face leaving the sanctuary of the room so instead sit down on the mat, knees drawn up in front of me, a soft navy towel wrapped tightly around me. The scent from the bath oils has soaked into my skin. I place my chin on the top of my knees and drink in the soothing aroma that transports me to a place where I feel safe again.

It feels as if I have been sitting in this same position for an eternity with my spine pressed up hard against the radiator, only shifting position when the skin on the back of my ribcage begins to burn. I do not want to feel, but equally neither do I wish to continue to endure the numbness that has enveloped me for so long. Pain is the only way that I can be sure I am still alive and I both fear and embrace it.

When I finally pluck up enough courage to leave the sanctuary of the bathroom, I find that daylight has already given way to darkness. There is something about the fading of the light that has always made me feel alone. Perhaps it is the thought of those long hours stretching out before me with no possibility of any interaction with another human, or simply the sense of fear that always returns to me when night descends, only to dissipate again with the first rays of dawn. I have been afraid of the dark since I was a child, when I came to fear the dark shadows that danced across my bedroom wall; the ominous cupboard in the corner of the room that could be hiding any number of terrors; the inexplicable noises from the sitting room located below my bed, where I was not allowed to enter after bedtime.

The night has long since been my nemesis; the foe I have never been able to defeat and I suspect that I never will. Night terrors that have plagued me since the age of five - a dark shadowy figure who tries to kill me in my bed - and even though I know that I am asleep and the image is not real, I am paralysed with fear. By the time I have fought to awaken from the dream, my sheets are drenched with sweat and my muscles ache from the contracting tension that has spread throughout my body. When I was a child, my screams echoed through the household, but no one came to check on me. Of course, now there is no one to hear my screams, which go unheard by any living creature besides Merlin. The feeling of absolute loneliness is unequivocal. Sitting in the darkness, clutching onto the thick duvet, waiting for my breath to settle; waiting for the shadows that are dancing across the walls to stop looking like the man who has just tried to murder me in my dreams. These night terrors continue to haunt my slumber and always I am left with the fear that one day they might come true.

The images of my night terrors are still fresh in my mind as I enter the darkness of my bedroom. The curtains are still closed from the last night that I slept here. I creep across the floorboards, as if fearing to waken a ghost, and fumble for the switch on the bedside light. Suddenly the room is filled with a comforting yellow glow and the familiarity of it soothes me. My eyes comb through the space, checking that all is in place; the mirror in the middle of the dressing table still sits at an angle; the wardrobe door is shut as always and my slippers are lined up next to the bed, waiting for their owner to get up in the morning. My attention is drawn to the pale pink bedspread, which covers the entire bed, pulled up over the crisp white pillows, corners neatly tucked into the mattress. Lying towards the foot of the bed, on top of the cover, is a pair of grey trousers, a white shirt, pale blue pullover and underwear, all neatly laid out as if they are waiting for me. A cold shiver runs down my spine, my breath quickens and the tiny hairs stand up along my forearms. I have no recollection of putting these clothes out and if I did not, who did?

Automatically I freeze, breath abated as I listen for any sounds that could alert me to the presence of someone else in the house, but there is nothing. From this distance I cannot even hear the detested clock that still sits pride of place in the centre of the mantlepiece in the front sitting room.

The house is too quiet. I suddenly realise that it has been several days since I last saw Merlin. Perhaps he too has deserted me. A jolt of fear flashes through me that perhaps he is lying injured somewhere, or trapped in a shed of a nearby garden, or has been taken by someone who could mean to harm him. Suddenly a wave of despair washes over me, I feel so completely exhausted and so utterly helpless that the possibility of leaving the house to look for my beloved cat does not even occur to me.

It has been many weeks since I have had any meaningful encounter with anyone outside of the house. It feels as if a lifetime has passed since I last exchanged a few pleasantries with the butcher's lad who comes to deliver the weekly order, or a few shrift words with the newspaper boy, who has once again forgotten to deliver the paper and in his haste has thrown it onto the front door mat as he passes on his way back to the newsagents. I cannot recall the last time I walked to the local bakery to buy fresh bread, or even just to the well-stocked corner shop to buy some extra eggs to bake a sponge cake. I have not noticed it happening, but my world has diminished, becoming smaller and smaller until it has shrunk into the house that has become my world. It is of course my own ineptitude that has resulted in chores being done over and over again, leaving little time for anything else. I miss those trips to the shops, passing the time of day with another human being had reminded me that I was not completely alone in the world and brought some relief from the overwhelming quiet stillness of the house.

As time passes and I hear no other sounds within the house, I begin to feel more confident that there is no one else here. Perhaps I am mistaken and forgot that I had put out the clothes. I unwrap the fluffy towel, placing it onto the bed next to the garments, then pick them up one by one and carefully dress, being mindful of the tender bruises around my ankles and inner thighs. When I am dressed, I move around the bed to stand in front of the mirror that sits on my mahogany dressing table. A gaunt, pale figure appears opposite me, shoulders rounded, as if she is trying to disappear into herself. I almost do not recognise her. I cannot bear to see the image any longer and turn away from the pitiful figure.

The floorboards creak under my weight as I move across the floor to the door. Tentatively I reach out and lightly place my hand over the brass door knob. My mind is in turmoil, I cannot decide if I should just stay in the room and allow myself the luxury of feeling safe for a while. Of course, this would be the easier option, but I steel myself to be brave once more and turn the handle until a sharp click echoes through the stillness. Slowly I pull open the door, afraid of what may be on the other side.

My heart thumps as I open the door and peer around it. The landing is empty. I pull back the door a little further so that I can pass through the gap, then I push through the small space, allowing it to gently close behind me. Quietly I pad across the thin carpet towards the top of the ornate mahogany staircase that I had always thought seemed far too grand for this modest sized house. I stand on the top step, hand gripping onto the smooth banister, which feels cool beneath my fingers. My weak legs reluctantly carry me down to the next step before I need to pause again. My strength returns with each movement and before long I have completed the journey to the bottom of the staircase.

Tentatively I place one foot onto the tiled floor in the hallway, followed swiftly by the other, then carefully sit down on the bottom step. The worn carpet seems thinner than ever under my bruised pelvis, making sitting almost unbearable. The house is quiet. I place my hands on top of my knees and observe the sounds of life outside of the house, a world where everyone else's lives have carried on, completely oblivious to the life that is falling apart inside. I listen intently to the passing cars, wondering where they are going and to the footsteps hurrying along the pavement on the other side of the wrought iron gate that marks the end of the property. I imagine people rushing home from a difficult day at work, desperate to return to the sanctity of their homes where they can forget about their troubles for a while. Nearby an infant in a neighbouring house has woken up and begins crying inconsolably.

I return my attention to the inside of the house again. The blanket of darkness that has descended feels heavier than ever. It weighs me down with the trauma of the past and the grief of knowing that my future will never be all that I dreamt it would be. I am unable to move, afraid that if I do, that something else bad will happen. Something that I have experienced more than enough of, enough for many lifetimes.

The noise from the infant suddenly stops. I picture in my mind the mother lovingly picking up the distressed child, holding it close to her chest, humming a soothing tune softly under her breath as she rocks it to sleep again. I cannot imagine that feeling of such acute trust for another human being, unconditional love that knows no boundaries, given freely without any expectation of reward. I understand of course that this is how a child should feel, but it is not an emotion that is familiar to myself. My mother was skilled at providing an illusion of love in front of neighbours and friends, but it was a shallow gesture with no substance and the hollowness of it echoed through my soul. Giving a performance of affection without true love or empathy leaves a bitterness, a jealously of the trickery, that you have not received the measure of attention that you deserve; an innocent child who has not asked for anything. This shallow façade of love leaves the child forever feeling they are not good enough, that they do not deserve to be loved and respected and nothing else can ever fill the chasm left by a chaotic childhood filled with fear and uncertainty.

Merlin suddenly appears from the kitchen to comfort me, in the same way that he always does when I am upset. He brushes up against my legs, his raggedy tail coiling around them like a snake around a tree. It is strange that he should appear at this time, as if he senses when I am in need of comfort. I place a hand onto the top of his head and gently stroke him, fingers curling around the back of his ears. He tolerates this for a while, then turns his back on me and saunters back into the kitchen where he disappears from view.

It is only when the outside world is quiet again, that I gingerly pull myself up and quietly creep back up the stairs, leaving the omnipresent ticking of the carriage clock behind. I do not bother switching on any lights, I know these stairs so well that I have no fear of misplacing my footing and in any case, the landing is lit by the most brilliant white moonlight shining through the stained glass window at the top of the stairs, leaving streaks of red and blue across the wall.

An overwhelming feeling of exhaustion suddenly

washes over me. My legs feel as if they are made of lead. I lift each one in turn up and place it firmly onto the step before repeating the action until I am once more at the top of the stairs. The carpet feels soft underneath my bare feet after the hardness of the tiled hallway floor. I pad across the landing to the door to my bedroom and gently push it open with the palm of my hand. Slowly I inch my way towards the bed then carefully climb on top of the bedspread, pulling over me the heavy blanket that I keep at the end of the bed.

And there I stayed all night, too exhausted from the events of the previous day to do anything other than allow the comforting numbness of sleep wash over me. That is, until the bleeding started. At first, it was just a trickle, the warm wet sensation waking me from my deep innocent slumber. At that point it was not enough for me to lose all hope, that realisation came later when I was forced from the bedroom, clutching weakly onto the wall as wave after wave of nauseous cramps rippled through me. It seemed as if my body would be torn apart, but of course it did not and after what felt like hours sitting on the bathroom floor, sobbing as I clutched onto my swollen belly, the physical pain subsided.

The pain of knowing that the child within me is now lost, is one that will stay with me for the remainder of my life, along with the uncontrollable rage that is now consuming me, that someone else has caused this.

CHAPTER EIGHTEEN

The house is encased in silence. The darkness comforts me with the knowledge that the dangerous part of the journey has by now been successfully navigated and that, as always, my meticulous planning has paid off. The girl is quiet. I watch as she looks around the small kitchen at the rear of the property, her vision having become adjusted to the dim light from the moon shining onto the cobbled back yard.

Her eyes comb through the space and eventually fall onto the spot where I am standing, silhouetted by the aluminium casement window that overlooks the small back yard. I can tell from the brightness of her eyes that she is afraid. Tentatively she smiles at me, hoping to glean whatever information she can from my reaction - to ascertain the type of person I might be, or the motive behind the situation she has found herself to be in. Often the fear of what is to come is worse than the actual event itself, though in this case, she is right to be afraid. She is controlling her emotions well though and I feel a small prickle of pride that my choice this time has been a good one.

I reach around to the other side of the rectangular wooden table and pull out one of the worn pine chairs, motioning for her to sit down. Gingerly she sits and places her hands flat onto the table. Her wrists are still bound and even in this dimmest of light, with the darkness only just being held back by the breaking dawn, I can see that the rope has been chafing at her soft, delicate skin.

'What is your name?'

'Dawn,' the girl stutters, her response betraying her attempt to appear more confident than she really is feeling.

'How old are you?' I ask softly.

'Sixteen,' she whispers. Her face crumples as it occurs to her that she may not see her seventeenth birthday, that she may never learn to drive, or graduate from school, wear a wedding dress or know the pain of childbirth. She cannot meet my eyes, as hers are filled with tears. She tries to prevent them from falling, but she cannot control her body from this most basic of functions and the tears cascade down her pale cheeks before dripping onto the table below.

The thought that I have the power to prevent this sweet, innocent child from having to go through all the heartaches of life is a comforting one. I understand enough of empathy to know that she will not of course appreciate my intentions and will instead only focus on loss, rather than what she will gain. She does not understand that she will be one of the lucky ones. She will never know the misery of growing old, having her days filled with the tedium of chores, and watching your mother slowly die from cancer. Nor will she feel the devastation of betrayal, when the only person you have ever trusted departs from your life as quickly as they arrived.

'I hope you like your new home,' I say quietly. The words are enough to stop her tears. She looks up at me, and I can see that a glint of hope has appeared in them, shining brightly in the hazy light. As soon as I say the words, I wish that I could take them back. I

have given her false hope that she might stay alive. I should not have done that.

Leaving the girl seated, her eyes following my every move, I walk around the table to the far end of the room, where there is a small lobby area leading to a downstairs cloakroom. In the centre of the lobby is the back door. I pull out a small silver key from my left trouser pocket, insert it into the keyhole and by pushing up on the handle at the same time, lock the door. The door is partially glazed with privacy glass on the top half, though the layers of dust and grime serve just as well to stop anyone from looking in. Even through the grime, I can see that the darkness is receding more quickly now as the sun rises higher into the sky. The back of the house is not overlooked, there is a high brick wall surrounding the yard but still, it is time to move her to a more secluded room where we will not be disturbed.

I return to the kitchen and squeeze past the table again. The girl's gaze is still transfixed upon me, her wide eyes brimmed with fresh tears that threaten to fall at any moment. She is still watching me as I stride across the room towards the door that is directly opposite her and leads out into the hallway. The door, which dates from the 1930's, has dropped slightly and scrapes across the tiled floor as I push it open. When it is only open half way, the door becomes stuck and cannot be opened any further, but no matter, the gap is large enough for me to squeeze through.

I push myself out into the dark hallway and towards the looming shadow of the staircase that dominates the narrow space. The staircase was once painted a glossy white, but has now darkened to a dirty yellow, matching the grimy patterned carpet on the steps. Underneath the staircase is a door. At first glance it is barely visible, it blends so well with the surrounding painted wood that encases the staircase. But once seen, it cannot be unseen again, however much someone may wish to. The key for the cellar door has been tucked underneath the carpet of the ninth step, for as long as I can remember. I push the tips of my fingers under the worn carpet, trying to quash my revulsion at the feeling of decaying fibres pushing up underneath my nails, as my fingers flail about, searching for the sensation of cold, hard steel. My efforts are rewarded by reaching deep inside the minute void that I have made by teasing the carpet away from the wooden step. Seconds later, I have successfully extracted a key between my fingertips.

A glance back at the girl tells me that my actions have not gone unnoticed. Her breathing has quickened, her pupils are now dilated as she stares wide-eyed in turn at both myself and the door. She knows. The girl knows what is to come.

CHAPTER NINETEEN

The next few days are a blur as I weep and rage in alternate cycles of self-deprecation and despair. The nauseous feeling of disgust at the violation to my body is ever present, with an overwhelming feeling of self-repugnance, as I chastise myself over and over again, for somehow failing to prevent the tragedy that unfolded a few days ago. It is this thought that torments me the most - that I cannot imagine how I will ever forgive myself for failing in the most basic of maternal duties; to protect the child I had only just discovered I was carrying.

During the last few days, I searched the house countless times for something with which to kill myself, but did not find any painkillers or poisons that could have allowed me to slip quietly away into the comforting arms of death and despite the deep chasm of despair that I was in, I could not bear to inflict further physical pain on myself. Eventually the overwhelming despair slowed to a quiet trickle then gradually ebbed away, leaving the same void of nothingness that has occupied my mind for so long now, that I can barely remember a time without it. It is almost a relief to be able to crawl back into the warm, comforting hole and leave behind all those overwhelming emotions and torturous thoughts that I can no longer bear to think about.

It is Monday morning when I finally manage to snap out of the blackness that shrouds me. I look out of the sitting room window at the sun, which is just beginning to peek above the rooflines of the terraced houses on the opposite side of the road. There are only a few lights on in the neighbouring houses. It is still too early for most of them to awaken and I imagine them curled up in their cosy, warm beds, trying to ward off the working week for a little longer.

I make my way through the quiet hallway to the kitchen and switch on the kettle to make a mug of strong tea. In the garden, the birds have already begun their sweet celebration of the new day, just as they did three sunrises ago. In an instant, the sound takes me back there again to the shed; my hands and feet are bound by rope, that has begun to chafe at my soft skin; my dry lips are pressed up against the roughness of the coarse hessian sack, sucking in the warm, stale air. I cannot breathe. The sack only allows for the shallowest of inhalations, and the fibres trap the exhaled air inside the narrow void, where oxygen levels diminish with every passing hour.

I concentrate on listening to the innocence of the birdsong, imagining them perched high up in the conifer tree behind the shed. The sound soothes me, slowing my breath down to a resting rate, quelling the panic that is rising within me, at the thought of being trapped there until my death. Such a thought often came to me in the shed.

The sound of a newspaper being roughly pushed though the brass letterbox and dropping innocuously onto the door mat below, grounds me; this singular, unspectacular, familiar sound is enough to jolt me from my hazy stupor. It is as if I have been in another place where time has stood still, then as suddenly as I have left, I am back again, safely returned to the present moment.

Automatically I wipe the palms of my hands, which are moist, against the top of my thighs, noticing the softness of the material. I turn away from the window and pad back into the hallway again. as I do so, my vision focuses on the rolled up object that is lying on the front door mat, one corner ripped from the force of being shoved through the small, rectangular opening. I crouch down, fingers outstretched, to pick up the object. I have forgotten not to overreach and the dull pain from the welts at the top of my inner thighs, throbs angrily, as if to chastise my forgetfulness. The sensation is yet another reminder of what happened three days ago, and I push it to the back of my mind. Gingerly I perch on the bottom tread of the stairs and place the newspaper on my lap. Carefully I unfold it, flattening it out over my knees and smoothing out the pages, just as I did as a child when unwrapping a birthday present.

It is there on the front page. I stare at the words over and over again, as if trying, yet failing, to comprehend their meaning. I do not need to read past the headline to know what the article contains, but I cannot help myself and my eyes devour each word in turn.

SUFFOLK HERALD

Morning Edition   Suffolk

Search Continues for Missing Girls

Suffolk police have confirmed that they are still searching for Annalise Taylor and Caitlyn Field, who vanished on separate occasions, close to the centre of town during the last few weeks. Neither of them are known to have contacts outside of the area, though the possibility of them running away has not been ruled out. Police are also considering if the vanishings of the two girls are in some way connected and if there could be a more worrying reason for their disappearance.

Measures Introduced To Tackle Vandals

The Council have confirmed extra funding to tackle the growing problem of vandalism that is blighting the town. Visitors to the town centre have complained about graffiti on the walls of shops in the new Buttermarket shopping centre. A community police officer will now patrol the area in the evening.

I sit motionless on the threadbare carpet of the bottom step, frozen again deep within my soul. I cannot fathom what it is that I am feeling, but I know that something about the newspaper article has triggered a reaction deep within me. Something about the story is familiar to me, though I do not know what it is.

On the other side of the front door, footsteps confidently approach, then stop at the top of the concrete path. A sharp clink reveals that a milk bottle has been placed into the white, metal framed bottle stand, followed by the dull clank as the empty one is removed. The reminder that the world is continuing with its normal daily life regulates my breathing once again and my pulse slows down to its normal resting pace.

The loud shrill of the telephone in the hallway startles me. For a moment I do not move, stunned into submission. Slowly, my mind registers the need for some kind of action and I shake myself from the shallow stupor that has descended over me. Stiffly I stand up, then carefully move towards the table near the front door. The shrill ring from the dark green phone still fills the air as I reach over to pick up the receiver.

'Hello,' I say cautiously.

'Hello, is that the Bonner residence?'

'Yes it is,' I reply, uncertain of where the conversation is heading.

'Hello, my name is Malcolm, I'm in charge of the accounts at the Co-op. It has been brought to my attention that your dairy bill has not been paid for the last three months.'

'Hasn't it? I don't know why that is,' I respond, puzzled by the conversation.

'I'm sorry but we're going to need to put your account on hold until the bill is paid off. Would you like to set up a payment plan?'

I stare at the telephone receiver as if not understanding the words I am hearing. It occurs to me that perhaps the call is a fake one, that someone is playing a prank on me. Without responding, I replace the receiver onto the cradle with a clatter, then return to the bottom step, where I pick up the paper again.

I stare at the newspaper that is lying on my lap. My eyes move downwards to the words underneath the headline, but my vision blurs, as if trying to prevent me from reading onwards. I persist, focusing on each word in turn, and read through line after line. My pulse races faster with every word that I read, my instinct is telling me that I know something about what has happened to those girls. Why can I not remember what it is?

Gently I fold up the newspaper again, smooth out the front cover, then place it back onto the doormat. I nestle back into the stair tread, feeling the hardness of the wood in the centre of my back. It seems a lifetime ago when I had last sat there, waiting for Alex, dreading the moment when I would hear the sound of a key turning in the latch, the creak of an old wooden door swinging open, the sound of footsteps clipping across a tiled hallway floor. Now it feels as if it were all a dream, one of my night terrors from which I cannot awaken that has suddenly gone, as if it were never there in the first place. I am not the same person I was the last time I had sat here on the step waiting for Alex. I am broken, but yet there is a tiny shard of hope beginning to tug at my heart.

I sit all day on the step, waiting, without knowing what I am waiting for. Frozen by all that has happened, and by the fear of what may come. It is only when the sun begins to set that I feel as if I can move again, the shards of ice in my soul melting. Streaks of orange, tinged with pink, penetrate through the stained-glass window of the front door, casting beams of colour onto the floor below. It looks so beautiful. So peaceful. I cannot recall when I last felt at peace. I cannot remember the last time I smiled or laughed. It is as if my mind has been numbed to all emotions except fear.

I do not notice the cold penetrating through my feet from the tiled floor, until the chill has begun to radiate up my shins and onwards toward my knees. The cold spurs me into movement and I stand up. My feet are so cold that I trip over the front door mat.

Automatically I thrust out a hand towards the banister to steady myself and hit my little finger on the newel post. A torrent of pain flashes through me. I cannot decide if I like the feeling of pain or prefer to be numb; the pain reminds me I am alive, that I have survived, but the empty void protects me from the memories I am not yet ready to face.

Unsteadily I make my way up the stairs. The light is fading rapidly and as always, the darkness leaves me with an uneasy feeling in the pit of my stomach. I cross the landing and switch on the bedroom ceiling light. Automatically my eyes flick through the room, checking that everything is in its place. My eyes settle on the wall behind the door. The dent in the dusk rose wallpaper takes me to a place I do not wish to go to; a shadow in the doorway; the stench of sweat soaked into a white shirt; the sharp odour of cheap whisky on the breath; the feeling of heaviness on top of me with no way to escape. Without thinking my hand cups my belly, then realising what I have done, I sink down into the threadbare carpet, unable to stop the memories of what happened in the shed from filling my mind. The consequences of that night are too much for me to bear right now. Steeling against my emotions, I push the thoughts from my mind and force myself to get up from the carpet and crawl into the warm bed.

I cannot sleep. My mind is restless, not from the events that have occurred over the last few days, but from the impudent thoughts that keep niggling at me. The words from the newspaper keep running through my head. I know they are important to me, but my mind is not allowing me to connect up the dots. I remember once hearing that the mind has a very clever way of protecting itself from memories that are too painful to acknowledge, but I know that there is something I need to remember, for if I do not, then another girl will go missing. I do not know how I know this, I just know it.

The darkness weighs heavily upon me with the burden of my mind and I can no longer stand to be alone with my thoughts. I reach out to switch on the brass lamp that is on the bedside table. The gentle yellow light calms my racing pulse, but it cannot soothe my mind. I throw back the heavy bedspread and sink my bare feet into the fluffy slippers that are in the same place next to the bed as they always are, just as Alex has taught me. Alex. There is something in the newspaper articles that makes me think of Alex. Perhaps it is Alex that my mind is trying to protect me from.

CHAPTER TWENTY

I cannot breathe. Sitting in the impenetrable darkness, the warm stale air trapped inside the cellar weighs heavily down onto my lungs. I cannot recall when or for what purpose grandfather had insulated and boarded out the cellar. Perhaps he had used it as a playroom? Yes of course, that's it, now I remember. It was a playroom, but not one for children with their innocent games and childish toys, but one for adults, with a different kind of game in mind, whose toys were not ones that a child should play with. The padlocked door was there to hide secret games from prying eyes, but it did not hide it from one curious child, who should have known better than to pry into matters that did not concern them.

A fleeting image comes to mind of a small child, creeping quietly down the stairs, one tread at a time, taking care to avoid the third from bottom step that always creaked, no matter how lightly it is trod upon, even by tiny, bare feet. It is night time and the house is quiet. Too quiet. A strange atmosphere has befallen the house that cannot be explained by the tense darkness. The child is scared of the dark. The child knows that they should be tucked up in bed, sound asleep, unaware of the anticipatory feeling that has descended upon the house. But the child is curious, it knows something is different, something has changed in its small world that has barely experienced life outside of the house. The journey through the darkness, past the sinister shadows that flicker across that vast hallway wall, is one that has been made often enough, but this is not like all the other times. This time there is no one downstairs. There are no peals of laughter coming from behind the closed living room door. Nor are there any strange grunting sounds that remind the child of the runt that had lived in the backyard until grandmother decided he was fat enough to eat.

The creature, which was still covered in soft downy fur, was pale pink, except for a splodge of dark brown on its right ear. Its stunted legs left its belly close to the ground, which resulted in mud being splashed up its underside, every time it rained. I had fed that pig every morning for three months, with scraps of cabbage, carrot scrapings, potato peelings - whatever morsel that grandmother was intending to throw away, went into a bucket near the back door.

Every morning I had eagerly put on my slippers ready to carry the heavy tin pail into the yard, the metal handle biting into the soft flesh of my young fingers, the sharp edge at the bottom of the pail, banging into my thin legs at the point where the navy blue dressing gown, which was too small, did not reach. Every morning when I opened the back door, the pig had run towards me as fast as his little trotters could carry him, squealing with delight at the sight of his breakfast. I still remember the way his furry nose ferreted amongst the kitchen slops to root out his favourite vegetable peelings, and the way his soft eyes gazed at me when I scratched him on his back after he had had his fill. And I still recall the way he had squealed when my grandfather had held him up in the air by his trotters and slit his throat; the way his *life force had pumped out of him and spread across the yard until his heart stopped beating; the way my grandmother had screamed at me to throw straw down onto the ground to mop up the blood before it stained the cobbles and later, the way the saturated straw emitted a rich, earthy odour as I gathered it up and threw it onto the compost heap. I remember that tiny pig as clearly as if it were here in front of me right now.*

And what of that small, curious, child, the one who was coming down the stairs in the dark, shuffling along a dark, empty hallway, poking its nose into things that were not their concern. Learning of things that they should not have seen. It was not the light from the living room that night that had caught the child's attention, but a bright yellow light that was coming from underneath the cellar door; the door that must always be kept locked, so that no one could accidently hurt themselves on the tools kept down there. The same door that was now open, allowing the faint sound of sobbing to penetrate through the thick blackness and reach the ears of a small child; a small child who should have been tucked up in bed, safe and sound; a small child who should not have been standing at the top of the wooden stairs, crouched down, peering inside the cellar; a small child who has seen something they should not have seen. Something their grandfather did not want to be seen. There was someone in the cellar, who was not supposed to be seen. Especially not by a small, curious child.

I stand up abruptly and shake my head, trying to rid myself of the unwanted memory that is intruding on my thoughts. The air is starting to cool a little now and I can breathe more easily again. I stretch out an arm and touch the wall in front of me, feeling the coldness of the damp bricks, the chalky sensation of crumbling dust between my fingertips. My hand continues on its journey down the wall until my fingers touch the smooth hard surface of the work bench. The one that grandfather made all those years ago, when he first fitted out the cellar to cater for his needs. His tools, which I sharpened and oiled yesterday, are already laid out on the bench, all in size order, equidistant apart from each other. My fingers continue up the wall above the bench, until they reach the smooth plastic of the light switch. I flick it on. Light fills the space, immediately replacing the oppressive darkness. The single white bulb hanging from the ceiling sways gently and the light from it as it moves gracefully from side to side, reflects onto the metal blade of the saw. I pick up the saw from its position in the centre of the bench and hold it up to the light to admire it. Automatically I run a finger down the serrated edge and watch, transfixed, as droplets of blood emerge from my finger-tip, then cascade onto the concrete floor below.

The faint whimper coming from the far corner detracts my attention from the droplets. I turn my head so that I can look behind me and discover the source of the noise. Of course! I have forgotten about her! She is still here. She is doing very well. The best yet.

CHAPTER TWENTY ONE

The article in the newspaper sparks the beginnings of an idea. Somewhere deep inside the depths of my mind, a memory has been triggered of listening to Alex recanting childhood tales, of visits to grandparents who lived in a two-up, two-down, mid-terraced house, close to the edge of town. Many an hour had passed sitting next to the fire in the front living room, listening to tales of a seemingly idyllic youth; throwing corn to the reddish brown hens who lived in the back yard; grandmother sitting by the aga, wearing a floral apron and burgundy-coloured carpet slippers to ward off the chill from the stone kitchen floor, making stews in the winter and quiche in the summer using eggs from the chickens. It did not occur to me until now, that Alex could be the beneficiary of the property from those childhood memories. There is a seed of thought needling at me, that Alex has something to do with the disappearance of the girls in the paper and if I am right, then Alex needs to be found.

My thoughts turn to the oak bureau in the dining room. I head down the hallway and through the second doorway on the left. On the other side of the door, set flush against the wall, is the solid oak bureau that has been in this house for as long as I can remember. My mother once told me, when she was tucking me up into bed one night, that my maternal grandmother had been widowed in her early forties and having no other source of income, had taken on a housekeeper role at a Georgian farmhouse close to the edge of town. The story was that when grandmother retired after twenty years of service to the Harrold family, she had been given the bureau as a gift. I had always believed that grandmother must have been well loved by the family to have been given something so expensive. Until, that was, when I read a newspaper clipping from the archive kept at the town library, dated a few weeks before grandmother retired..

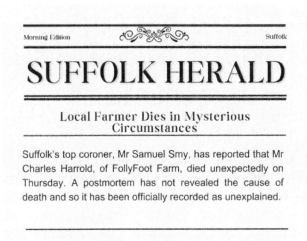

Morning Edition   Suffolk

SUFFOLK HERALD

Local Farmer Dies in Mysterious Circumstances

Suffolk's top coroner, Mr Samuel Smy, has reported that Mr Charles Harrold, of FollyFoot Farm, died unexpectedly on Thursday. A postmortem has not revealed the cause of death and so it has been officially recorded as unexplained.

I recall being told that the reason for my grandmother being given the bureau was that the family could no longer bear to see the piece of furniture as it had once stood in Mr Harrold's study, where he had spent many an hour going through the accounts and other such paperwork related to the farm business. My mother never told me how Mr Harrold had died, but another newspaper article revealed more detail than the original coroner's report.

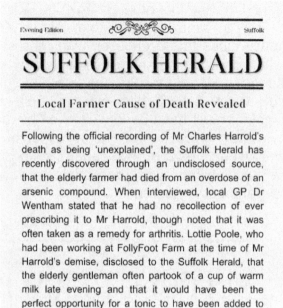

A subsequent article revealed that Mr Harrold had tried and failed to rid the family of a vast debt that had been built up by his brother's gambling losses and that when he died, the family were on the verge of bankruptcy. The coroner had given an open verdict of Mr Harold's death, as although there had been just cause for suicide, being a close friend of the family, he knew of the life insurance policy Mr Harrold had taken out less than one year before his death, and of the penalty clause that would forfeit the insurance in the event of the policy holder committing suicide. The last of the newspaper cuttings relating to the matter was an advertisement for an auction at FollyFoot Farm.

SUFFOLK HERALD

Auction at FollyFoot Farm

An auction is due to take place on Saturday, September 9 at FollyFoot Farm, where the contents of the main house are to be sold, along with some of the outbuildings and land surrounding the FollyFoot House. To be included in the auction are:

- Oak dining room table and 8 chairs
- Dark oak desk, bureau and book case
- Teak dressing table and stool
- 3 chandeliers

The auction will be conducted by Mr James Fitchett and will begin at 9am.

As the bureau had been included in the list, the town gossips had ruinously concluded that my grandmother must have somehow stolen the valuable item of furniture, even though no substance could be given to the accusations or as to the method of how a portly woman in her early sixties could possibly manage to carry a heavy piece of furniture nearly two miles to her home without anyone noticing. Of course, it had been a clerical error, but the smear on grandmother's good name remained intact and she could not find any further work after that and had instead relied on her life savings to keep her adequately fed and housed.

The small, iron key is always kept in the keyhole to the bureau, for there is nothing of any value in there to warrant locking it. I pull open the top drawer, noticing the pleasing sound of the wood as it moves smoothly over the runners, despite its lack of use.

Inside, there are several stacks of documents. I pick up a piece of paper from the top of the pile, unfold it and skim through the contents, then discard it onto the threadbare carpet below. I repeat the process and soon the room is littered with white paper, as if a light snow fall has blanketed the room unseen during the night. I continue until every single piece of paper from every drawer has been emptied from the cabinet. There is nothing there.

Sitting down amongst the crumpled letters, envelopes and old utility bills, I rack my brains as to where else I should look. The bedroom. It is the only place it could be, except for the shed of course and I cannot bear to contemplate going back into that space again.

I stretch out my legs, which have become numb from sitting on them, and wait impatiently for the pins and needles to subside. It seems as if my soul is as numb as my legs. I do not think I can even cry, I feel nothing, as if I no longer exist. Perhaps I am no longer alive? Perhaps I was killed after all and am now a ghost, no longer capable of feelings, trapped in this vacuous chasm, unable to move forwards, or backwards. Unable to be at peace.

A sudden noise stirs me from my stupor. For a moment I cannot work out what the noise is. There it is again, a loud banging noise that seems to be coming from the front of the house. Someone is knocking on the front door.

'Hello, is anyone in?' a voice calls from beyond the door.

I am paralysed by indecision, not knowing whether or not I should open the door. The noise comes again.

'Hello Beth, its Joanne from next door.'

I creep into the hallway, to see a stocky shadow on the other side of the glass. The letterbox opens, and two eyes try to peer in through the narrow gap, but it is dark in the hallway and they will not see much of interest. Abruptly the flap of the letter box is let go and snaps back into place. A loud sigh comes from the other side of the door then the noise ceases as suddenly as it arrives and the footsteps clip along the path once more, telling me that the person has left.

An object on the top of the bureau catches my attention. My eyes focus on the light blue box sitting in the centre of the piece of furniture. For a moment my mind is hazy and cannot fathom what it is, but soon the fog clears and I realise that it is my sewing kit. I reach up and clasp onto the object, but it slips from my grasp and clatters onto the floor below, spilling its contents across the rug. I stoop down to pick up the box, and in the process, I prick myself on a large darning needle that has fallen onto the rug beside the sewing kit. The sharp needle sinks into the soft skin on the underside of my forefinger. I watch as a droplet of bright red blood appears amongst the ridges of my finger, adorned by the 18 carat opal ring that once belonged to my mother. The droplets of blood run down my finger and onto the gold ring, where it spreads out and covers the surface of the metal, washing over it as if to cleanse it of its past mistakes. I watch until the bright red droplets stop forming on the surface of my skin, then stand up straight again, using the bureau to lean on.

Suddenly I feel exhausted, as if all the emotions from the past few days have flooded into me at the same time, swirling about in my head, screaming at me with no way of escape. I traverse the hallway and slowly make my way up the stairs. I am too exhausted to ignore the need for sleep any longer and fling myself on top of my bed, pulling the blanket that is always at the bottom of the bed, over me. As I slip into a peaceful dream-like state, I think I see a tall, lanky figure leaning against the doorframe, a shadow against the landing light. I know that I am alone in the house and therefore my mind must be playing tricks on me, but the image is so lifelike that for a moment I doubt myself, before allowing the weariness to overcome me and slip into the sanctity of sleep.

CHAPTER TWENTY TWO

It is daylight when I wake. I feel as if I have slept for a hundred years and that I could sleep for a hundred more, but I cannot do so, for I have too much to do. I must find Alex. The police are looking for anyone who knows something about the young girls' disappearance, but they do not yet know about Alex. I do.

It was not just Alex that I dreamt of last night, but of the child who has not been given the opportunity to live. I do not care for all that I have been through, all that I have endured, all that I have lost, but to kill an innocent child is unforgivable. Something deep inside of me has been unleashed, a strength that I never knew existed, an anger that has been suppressed for so long I had forgotten it were there. These last few days have been a torrent of emotions, of memories I do not ever wish to recall, of physical pain that I thought would never cease. But now it is as if the rainclouds have lifted and the sun is shining strong through the grey clouds, pushing them away with such vigour that they will never dare return. Now I have clarity of mind; I know what I need to do. I just need to figure out how to do it.

I swing my legs over the edge of the bed and carefully stand up. Dizziness washes over me. I am weak from lack of sustenance, I need to eat, to gain my strength again. Quietly I pad downstairs, as if afraid of awakening the evil spirit that has haunted these four walls for so long. I am certain that Alex is no longer here, but still, the fear is always with me.

Through the glass window above the front door, I can see that the sun is high above the rooftops, nestled amongst pillow-like clouds. The hallway is bathed in a warm light, but the rooms at the rear of the house stay hidden from the sun for much of the day. I pass through the hallway and into to the darkness at the rear of the property. The door to the kitchen is partially open, in the same position that I left it yesterday. I pass through the threshold and reach out with my left hand for the light switch. The overhead strip light ignites with a faint buzzing. The familiarity of the sound both comforts and repels me in equal measure from the memories that are held within this space. The floor is cold as ever and I chastise myself for not having the foresight to bring my slippers, which are still upstairs, lined up next to my bed. I squeeze past the pine table to open the cupboard above and begin to rifle through it in desperate hope, knowing fully that the stocks have not been replenished this week as I would normally have done. As predicted, my effort goes to waste, there is nothing even remotely palatable in the cupboard. I close the door again and survey the worktop below.

Rummaging through the breadbin I am rewarded with three quarters of a wholemeal loaf that has been there for several days. Steeling myself, I cut off the mouldy parts of the loaf and discard them into the nearby bin. I slice off a thick chunk and place it under the grill to brown. From the fridge, I extract the butter dish and a pot of strawberry jam and place them onto the worktop next to the small plate that I have taken from an overhead cupboard. I pick up the kettle and place it under the tap in the kitchen sink, then replace it and switch it on. I catch myself from pulling out two mugs from the dresser and choose just one to place onto the table. The teapot is as always sitting on the worktop close to the kettle, awaiting use. I stare at it for a moment, then hastily pick it up and push it to the back of the cupboard where I keep all the household items I do not like, and vowed that I would never use again.

The mug of sweetened tea and hot-buttered toast replenishes my energy levels sufficiently well for me to continue with my search. I head back upstairs and stand outside the closed door to the front bedroom. I imagine that there is someone inside, lying prone along the bed, still fully clothed from a drunken evening at the pub. I pluck up the courage to prove my imagination to be wrong, and reach out to place a hand on the brass door knob, leaving it there for a moment as I listen out for any movement within. Of course, there is nothing, only silence. Berating myself sternly for the foolish thought, I firmly twist the handle and push the door inwards at the same time, with the door creaking in protest.

It is dark inside the room. The curtains are still drawn and the sole source of light comes from the sun, which is just peeking through the central gap where the fabric does not quite meet. Automatically my eyes are drawn to the bed, as if half expecting to see someone there, but of course the room is empty. Striding across the whitewashed floorboards, I pull back the curtains, allowing the bright sunlight to flood in. A quiet stillness blankets the room, as if the evil that once resided within the walls has been washed away, cleansed by the brilliance of the light. The knot in the pit of my stomach that I did not know was there until now, dissipates. The tautness of my jaw muscles relaxes, as the underlying feeling of terror that has been haunting me for the past few days, is unexpectedly replaced with one of peace.

As my vision rapidly adjusts to the brightness of the room, I begin to comb through the space, my eyes resting on each familiar object in turn; the half tester mahogany bed with matching bedside table; the ornate brass lamp with its shade that was once a brilliant dark green but has been faded by the sunlight to a washed-out jade; the blanket box at the bottom of the bed that had been bought from a second-hand shop by my mother to house the plethora of rough pink blankets that would cover all of our beds in the winter. I vividly recall the purchase of the blanket box one autumnal Saturday morning, much to the disappointment of my father, who had intended to spend the money at the races that afternoon.

One wall of the bedroom is over-shadowed by an immense teak wardrobe that my mother loathed vehemently. I traipse across the room again, floorboards creaking underneath my feet. Grabbing hold of the tarnished iron key in the keyhole, I turn it with a satisfying click then pull both doors open fully. Inside, long-sleeved shirts, trouser and jackets, are all neatly pressed and lined up in order, starting on the left-hand side from the darkest colours and ending on the right with the lightest. I reach out to feel behind them in case there is anything hidden, then run my hands over the bottom of the wardrobe, noting the roughness of the wood under my soft skin.

Above the hanging rail is a shelf that runs across the width of the wardrobe. Four plain, cardboard boxes sit on top of the shelf, lined up equidistant from each other. I stretch up to pull down one of the boxes and place it gently onto the thin bedside rug.

Removing the lid reveals that there are documents inside. I take one out and read it carefully before placing it onto the rug beside my feet. Most of the documents consist of household bills, the remainder comprise insurance papers for a car that I do not recognise. I gently place them back into the box and replace it back onto the shelf. The next two boxes are similar, containing only bills and receipts.

The third box at first glance appears to be a repetition of the other boxes. I take out the paperwork at the top of the box and there underneath, is a small brown bag, its top neatly folded over. Gingerly I unfold the bag and pull it open. Tipping the bag upside down, the items tumble out one by one and scatter across the rug. I pick up the object nearest to me to inspect it more closely. It is a small silver bangle ornately engraved on the outside. Sitting down cross-legged on the rug, I turn the bangle over again and again in my fingers, hoping that it will jog my memory, but it remains unfamiliar to me and I place it back down again. Lying next to the bangle is a gold-plated locket, that is tarnished on the back. I unfasten the clip and open it up to reveal a black and white photograph of a small white dog. The last item from the bag is a silver dragonfly hairclip, studded with dark blue stones that look like sapphires. I pick it up, feeling the coldness of the metal, and run a finger along the stones, their smoothness evokes a distant memory of a pebble I once found on the sand being rhythmically washed by the incoming tide. My parents had taken us to the coast every summer for five years, idyllic days of making sandcastles and searching for pretty shells amongst the stones, of shallow pools hidden amongst the rocks, the water as clear as glass. It was such a delight to find one, like opening a Christmas present, you never knew quite what you would find resting on the golden sand; a piece of seaweed or a mermaid's purse, or if we were really lucky we might find a starfish trapped there by the outgoing tide. I can still smell the fresh salty water, feel the biting wind as it whips through my hair. I loved that place and every moment I had spent there. Until the day that is, when my brother died. Out there in the bitter blue-grey sea.

I put the hairclip back into the paper bag, along with the locket and bangle, then fold over the top again, gently pushing out the wrinkles until the paper is smooth. I put the bag back into the box and pull the lid on again. The box feels heavier now than when I first pulled it down from the shelf, perhaps the puzzling contents are weighing heavily on my mind. I stretch up and place the box back alongside the others on the top shelf, then take a step back to consider all that I have found. I do not understand why these objects are here in this house, but somehow, I know they are important.

Closing the heavy wardrobe doors again, my attention is brought back to the bed that dominates the centre of the room. I pad across the worn rug and perch on the edge of it. The mattress sags underneath my weight, the creaking springs heralding the presence of an unexpected visitor. The sound reminds me of the night my brother and I were caught jumping on his bed.

'Hey Beth, get into the boat, there are sharks in the sea.'

'Help me up then,' I had replied, grinning as I looked up at my brother from where I was sitting, cross-legged on the swirly carpet. I thrust a hand out, stretched upwards towards the bed.

'I can't Beth, you're too heavy!'

'I'll clamber up the ladder then!' I had replied,

pulling myself up by the sheet that was hanging over the side of the bed. Once on the bed, we had stood in the centre of it, giggling and pushing each other, daring ourselves to fall back into the shark-infested waters that comprised the bedroom carpet.

I still recall the shock on my brother's face as the slats beneath the mattress broke, springs tearing through the thin blue fabric as if it were paper. I certainly did not forget the look on mother's face, when she shoved open the bedroom door, curious as to the source of the peals of laughter that were seldom heard in the house.

'What the hell is going on here,' she had demanded, her bulging face reddening deeper by the second.

'We're just playing mum,' I had replied meekly, knowing that whatever I answered would anger her.

'Really, it looks to me as if you've been doing something you shouldn't have and now you've broken the bed that cost your dad a week's wages.'

I could not respond as I stared into her eyes, flashes of anger glinting in the dim light. 'Not going to speak now, are we? Well, that's not going to help is it. And don't think you'll be allowed to get away with this because you won't.'

We were not allowed to eat anything other than bread and butter for five days after that particular incident and the threat of an even worse punishment was enough to curtail our childish imaginations for a lifetime.

The memory fades and I am back in the room, still perched on the edge of the bed, both feet firmly planted on the fake fur rug that has yellowed with age into a dull beige. Releasing a long drawn out breath, I stand up and begin to move towards the door. As I stride across the centre of the rug, a dull creak comes from the floorboard underneath my foot, which sounds different from all the others. I crouch down and pull back the rug. The central board is a richer colour than the surrounding ones, which have been bleached by the sun and is only half their length. The board has been replaced. A nail is missing at one end of the board.

I search the room for something that could be used to lever it up with and locate a pencil that is lying on the top of the bedside table next to a small pad of yellowing paper. Pushing the tip of the pencil into the small hole that should house a thin nail, I push down onto it and force the board upwards just far enough for me to get my finger tip underneath. With a little more pressure, the board pivots at a right angle, leaving just enough room for a small hand to reach into the chasm and pull out the cloth bag that is hidden deep inside.

My fingers tremble as I unfold the top of the bag and pull out an A5 sized leather document folder. I unwrap the leather strap and allow the bag to open of its own accord, the concertina cardboard relaxing in the absence of any ties. Peering inside, I see a wad of documents that are folded in half. I pull them out and place them onto my lap. As I do so, a key drops out from the centre of the bundle, where it has been carefully hidden. It is a small, unremarkable brass key that has tarnished with age, the sort that could have once been used for a back door. I place it to one side and open out the document folder, then begin to rifle through the papers until I find a Last Will and Testament. I skim through the neatly written document until I find what I am searching for; the address of a small Victorian two up two down terraced house - 6 Ivry Street. Now I know where to find Alex, but the question is what do I do next?

CHAPTER TWENTY THREE

Morning Edition Suffolk

SUFFOLK HERALD

Is there a Serial Killer in Suffolk?

Suffolk police have reported that another teenage girl has disappeared from the town. Fifteen year old Dawn Cooper was last seen walking her dog in Seaton Park in the early hours of Sunday morning. The dog was later found wandering the streets and the alarm was raised that the girl was missing. Police have initially concentrated their search around the park and nearby streets, but have now widened their door-to-door search to neighbouring districts. Police have urged anyone who might have seen Dawn, who is described as 5 feet tall with shoulder length brown hair and was last seen wearing a red coat, to contact them urgently.

The similarities between the disappearance of three teenage girls in the area, has led local CID to consider if the cases could be related. Residents of the town are calling for the disappearances of Dawn Cooper, Annalise Taylor and Caitlyn Field to be treated as a murder enquiry, expressing their concern that a serial killer could be at large. The Suffolk Herald has learnt that Scotland Yard has now been called in to help with the investigation, which is on a scale unheard of before in this quiet part of the County.

Is this your Dog?

A dog has been found loose in Seaton Road. is this your dog? if so, contact Suffolk police on 276666

So, it seems that the police are beginning to understand what is happening. It will not be long now before they learn of my work. It is a pity that I will not be here to take pride in all that I have achieved, but I can feel in my bones that it is nearly time. Death is so

close now, that I can almost feel its fetid breath upon me. The thought makes me shiver, as if I have been touched by an icy tendril deep within the carcass of my soul; for there is little left inside of me now, that bears any resemblance to the person I was once. I cannot bear to remember the days before I became the creature that I am now, the days before my innocence was torn from me. Even now, with death following so closely behind I cannot bring myself to think of what has long since passed.

Sinking back against the cold, damp wall, I feel the hardness of the bricks pressing into my spine. It is an action that I have performed many times and the familiarity of the sensation comforts me. Automatically, I turn to gaze across the room to the wooden workbench that has been so pivotal in my life. This is the place where I learnt the lessons I needed to be taught. By the time my grandfather had finished teaching me all about his version of love, I had banished all feelings from me. I had become a ghost.

I can still recall the pleasure I had felt as pain was inflicted upon me, for it was the only reminder that I was still alive. It gave me a glimmer of relief from the numbness that shrouded my carcass. Of course, I did not understand back then, that grandfather's actions were not born out of love, but from a deep, uncontrollable desire to inflict misery on another human being. I did not know that his kind of love was wrong, that his actions would set me on a course far removed from the path of my school friends. I did not understand at that time, that this was a turning point in my life from which there was no going back. The lessons were taught with vigour and precision and the pupil understood them well. Grandfather's lessons became forever ingrained in my inner psyche, the very core of my soul, which withered and decayed, replaced by only a shell of a child who could feel nothing but pain.

I can almost understand my grandfather's actions, his belief in doing what he thought was right by teaching me the way he had been taught; the same way he had taught my father. But what I could not understand was the way my mother had turned her back on me and pretended it was not happening. What I could not banish from my memory was the image of my father, standing in the doorway to his bedroom, leaning against the painted white frame that had yellowed with age, watching as grandfather led me meekly down the stairs, still wearing my favourite dark blue pyjamas that were peppered with silver stars and reminded me of the night sky, down into that cold, dark cellar.

I shake off the memory. There is no point in remembering the past now and in any case, I must focus on the present. My work here is nearly done. I am achieving what I set out to do, learning all that I can from my life's journey. I know that it is almost time for me to leave this world and all the cruelty within it. I will not be sorry to do so, for this life has only shown me pain and unkindness. First though, before I depart from this world to the next, I must pass on the lessons that were taught to me, all those years ago. And so I am back in the cellar, but this time, I am not the pupil, but the teacher.

The steps creak under my nubuck brogues as I make my way up the open staircase. At the top, I pause to push open the wooden door that leads into the hallway. I am so lost in my thoughts, reminiscing of the past, fantasising of the future, that I do not hear the small whimper coming from behind me as I turn off the light, then firmly shut the door and fix the *padlock into place again.*

I wander into the kitchen, which is bathed in the darkness that I am now so accustomed to, with only the dim crescent moon to light my path. I pull back a chair, its wooden feet scraping across the tiles and sit down, then place my hands onto the table in front of me. The coolness of the melamine beneath my weathered fingers is refreshing and brings me back to the present, taking me away from the darkness of my past, that even now I cannot bear to remember.

It is quiet. In the hallway I can hear the rhythmic ticking of a clock, the omnipresent sound that has echoed throughout my living memory. The teak clock that has always hung on the wall opposite the staircase since I was a child, perhaps even before I was born. Tick, tick, tick. The rhythm that is so familiar has never changed, never altered, never ceased.

It seems that the outside world is sleeping, just as it was when I was a child and had made that first lonely journey into the cellar. Just as it was when I was given my first lesson and no one heard my screams. Just as it did when I became a ghost, walking through this world unseen, unnoticed by those who walk beside me, my cries unheard, my voice once loud, now silenced.

My eyes automatically fall to the newspaper that is still lying on the table, neatly folded into thirds, as I was taught to do. For a moment I feel as if I am a child again, sitting at the kitchen table, grandfather beside me, showing me yet again how to fold the newspaper then add it to the pile next to the aga so that it can be used to light the burner. But I am no longer a child and everything has changed; the house is empty of the ghosts of my past and I have done what I needed to do to free myself from the chains that bound me for so long and kept me silent of the horrors buried deep within. Now, at last, I have been heard, I have been noticed. I have lived disregarded by society, but my work will mean that I will not leave this world unseen.

And so it is that I now sit here in the kitchen that was once my grandmother's and wait - I wait for you to find me, for I know that you will. There is no escape from death.

CHAPTER TWENTY FOUR

A loud noise echoes through the stillness of the house with such suddenness, that I almost drop the document I am holding. I freeze, waiting to see if the noise will occur again, or if the usual turgid silence will resume. There it is again. I listen hard and this time I manage to deduce that the noise is coming from the front door and that someone is standing on the other side of it.

I creep across the landing towards the stairs. I cannot decide if I should pretend there is no one at home or open the door to discover who is knocking on it with such vigour, that the sound strongly reverberates through the foggy street. On the other side of the adjoining wall, a creaking noise informs me that my neighbours have opened their front door and muffled voices tell me that my neighbours are now conversing with whomever is on the front path. I strain to hear but cannot quite catch what is being said. Moments later, the sound of the neighbours' door being firmly shut echoes through the building, leaving an eerie silence in its wake.

Softly I pad down the stairs, nausea rising in my throat. My heart thumps so quickly that it feels as if it will burst out of the cage that protects it. I try to quell my fear by soothing myself with the platitude that the danger has now passed, that the visitor has been placated by my neighbours. Creeping down the stairs, I slink into the comforting darkness of the shadows, which are enveloping the hallway now that the sun is beginning to set. There is a terse silence, an anticipation that something unwanted is about to occur. As the light fades, a feeling of anxiety grows within me that I cannot shake off. Something is wrong.

As I am passing the front door, a sudden noise comes from the other side. I halt mid stride, muscles clenched in anticipation of the next movement. Softly I move across the dark hallway, taking care to avoid the beam of light from the moon, that is peeking through the half-crescent window above the front door. I pad across the cold tiles and step over the threshold of the sitting room. Immediately my taut body is calmed as I step into the comforting darkness.

There it is again; the clipped shudder of a brass door knocker being tapped confidently against the plate beneath. Craning my head around the door frame, I catch sight of a tall shadow through the stained-glass window. My heart begins to thump again, bile returning into the base of my dry throat. I cannot move, paralysed by indecision. If I just keep quiet, surely they will go away. Won't they?

Without warning, the brass letterbox in the centre of the door is flung open, its hinges whining at the suddenness of the movement. The whites of two eyes appear in the dark void, blinking to adjust to the dimness of the hallway. Momentarily the eyes connect with mine. The decision has now been made for me.

'Hello, my name's PC Martin. Please can you open the door.'

Gingerly I place one foot behind the other and creep backwards into the sitting room, wincing as the floorboards creak beneath my weight. The noise is so loud in the stillness of the house that the police officer must certainly have heard it. Soundlessly, I open the top drawer of the bureau, lift out the pile of papers in the centre of the space, then carefully slot in the Will and Testament. I place the papers back in the same spot, then noiselessly close the drawer again before reaching across to flick on the table lamp that sits on the side table next to the bureau. Then, as if I have only just heard the knock at the door, I purposely stride into the hallway.

The light is beginning to fade rapidly. I switch on the reproduction Tiffany ceiling light, that matches the lamp in the sitting room.

'Can I help you?' I ask, opening the front door. Behind the door, the police officer is standing motionless, fist drawn back in readiness to knock again. Automatically I shrink back, conditioned to respond to such a threat, even if it is unintentional. My reaction does not go unnoticed and the outstretched fist is slowly lowered then placed back alongside PC Martin's thick waist. I watch as he unfurls his taut hand, relaxing it to reflect his casual smile.

'Hello, thank you for answering the door. It doesn't seem as if many of your neighbours are at home today. We're talking to everyone in the area about the girls who have gone missing,' PC Martin explained.

I open the door a little wider, the hinges protesting at the movement. My lips feel dry. I run my tongue over the bottom lip, feeling the cracked skin beneath. Suddenly I realise that I am thirsty. I cannot remember when I last had a drink.

'I'm thirsty. I need to get a drink of water.' My voice wavers, which elicits a sympathetic smile from the police officer. I turn around, leaving the front door ajar and move back down the hallway towards the kitchen, which is now encased in darkness. My legs are trembling but hold up long enough for me to reach the door to the kitchen, where I clutch onto the painted frame, my fingers whitening with the force of my grip. I bite down onto my cracked bottom lip, trying to suppress the sob that is coming from somewhere deep within my soul. They are looking for Alex.

Indecision washes over me once again. Could I possibly dare to trust this person and tell them what I suspect about Alex, or do I keep my thoughts to myself? Although I feel certain that I am right, I have no real proof to support my suspicions and I am not sure that I will be believed.

Behind me, someone is clearing their throat. A sharp glance reveals the forgotten police officer still standing at the threshold, waiting patiently for my return. Tentatively I smile to acknowledge my awareness of his presence, then I turn again and step over the oak carpet step into the kitchen.

Eyes facing forward, I draw in a deep breath and slowly release it again in a steady flow. After a few slow, deep mouthfuls of air, my heart rate slows and the wave of dizziness that washed over me moments before, gradually subsides. I compose myself, then move across the kitchen to the sink, where I quickly fill a glass with fresh water and gulp down mouthfuls of the cool liquid. When my thirst has been satiated, I retrace my steps to the front door again and plaster a fake smile onto my face.

'Sorry about that, how can I help you?'

'As I said, we're looking into the disappearance of Annalise Taylor, Caitlyn Field and Dawn Cooper, whose families are extremely worried about their safety, as are the police. So, we're knocking on all the doors in this area as it's close to where they all disappeared.'

'I imagine their families must be very distraught. Could they have run away? It's not unheard of for teenage girls to disappear, perhaps they headed off on a train to London, met up with boyfriends there?'

'We've checked and there's no sign of them either buying a ticket or getting onto a train.'

I nod sympathetically, though in truth I have no idea how these girls' families are feeling and neither do I wish to contemplate their fate, for my instinct is telling me that somehow Alex is involved. I flash my sweetest smile at the officer, trying to appear empathic to hide the numbness that I feel within. A year ago, I could have mustered up some platitude of sympathy, but the void that has been growing within me, has pushed away any notion of empathy and left a dark cloud that has smothered all that was once good and kind, leaving an emotionless pit in its wake, of the kind that there is little hope of escaping.

My thoughts are interrupted by a hand waving something white in front of me. I focus on the small, rectangular objects, which gradually come into focus, to reveal the images of the three girls who have gone missing. I assume from the way that PC Martin is waving the photographs at me, that he would like me to look at them.

I grasp hold of the photo on the left and hold it between my petite fingers so that I can study it more closely. Although the photo is in black and white, it is easy to deduce that the slim built girl has shoulder length hair of a deep brunette. The girl has a carefree smile, without an ounce of hatred within her. A hand-written scrawl in the margin of the second photograph, identifies the figure as being Dawn Cooper. Only her head is visible, with her bouncy curls that cascade down her back and a beaming smile. Both girls look familiar to me. Perhaps I have seen their pictures somewhere, probably in the newspaper. The third girl looks similar to the others, though her sparkling eyes cannot belie her intelligence.

'I'm sorry, I haven't seen them,' I say to PC Martin, who is still waiting expectantly on the front path.

'Is there anyone else in your household who might have seen them?'

'There's no one else here. I'm alone.' The house suddenly feels very cold and lonely. It is silent except for the omnipresent ticking of the clock, which seems to be getting louder and louder, until it fills my head with such sounds that I can no longer think. I blink back the tears that have begun involuntarily to flow down my cheeks then bite my tongue sharply, to prevent any more from forming. Handing the photographs back to the officer, my smile widens in a way that tells him that this conversation is now over.

'Well, thank you for your time. If you do remember seeing the girls or recall hearing anything unusual on the days that they disappeared, please ask for me at the police station.'

'Of course.' This time my smile is genuine, I am glad that he is leaving and that the awkward questioning can now cease.

I stand at the threshold to my house and watch as PC Martin strides back up the narrow path again, the heels from his polished shoes clipping against the concrete. As he walks, his head is momentarily cast downwards, pen poised above the list he has pulled out from the inner pocket of his coat. I continue to watch as he turns left onto the public footpath and strides off towards another neighbours house. I feel relieved though I do not understand why. Surely I want Alex to be caught? After all, something very bad has happened and it needs to be stopped. This was my opportunity to speak up, so why did I not tell the police about my suspicions?

CHAPTER TWENTY FIVE

I cannot just sit here like some pathetic dog awaiting its fate. This is not how I have been brought up, how I have been taught to behave. I must fight - fight against what I know is inevitable. I cannot allow death to just walk into the room and take me whenever it chooses to. I will not allow it. Death does not have the right to determine my fate, only I have. It is my life after all.

I stare out into the back yard until the darkness shields my view. The streetlamps on the nearby pavement flicker into life, their weak beams casting shadows along the alleyway that runs behind the row of houses that are located on the same side as the house where I am now residing - 6 Ivry Street. The narrow, cobbled path that runs down the centre of the alleyway and is flagged on both sides by brick-built walls, is littered with discarded items that cannot fit into the rubbish bins, which stand forlornly outside each gate like sentries on guard duty. The yellow beam from the street lamp at the end of the alleyway, highlights every piece of trash that litters the path, as if trying to shame the perpetrators who have so carelessly discarded them. After midnight, the streetlights are switched off by the Council in an effort to save money, and the detritus from local residents' lives are once more hidden from sight. The impenetrable darkness it leaves behind has served me well, in ensuring that my comings and goings have remained unseen. I have no need for such care now though, for this will be the last time that I make this particular journey.

Poignantly I open the back door of my grandfather's terraced house and close it gently behind me. This is the final time that I will be in this place, standing here in the centre of this rectangular brick-lined yard. The light of the quarter moon shines a spotlight onto each part of the yard, bringing forth a myriad of long forgotten memories; the washing line where grandmother hung her billowing sheets still sags across the yard, the wooden pole that once held it off the ground, stands at a tilt against the far wall; the old outhouse still occupies the far corner of the yard, complete with toilet and wooden seat, the metal box below it has decayed through years of unuse. Butting up to the outhouse is a small brick-built outbuilding, where the half open stable door is banging gently against the brickwork. I can still smell the slurry from the pigs, see them wriggling and squealing as they are taken into the dimly lit coal shed whose metal door, when closed, blocks out every ounce of light. I can still hear their screams as my grandfather slit their throats and the ensuing silence afterwards that told me that they were now dead.

My eyes follow my train of thoughts and halt at the unmistakable shadow of the coal shed, its corrugated tin roof partially lit by the moon's lonely light. I close my eyes, squeezing them tightly shut. I do not wish to remember what else happened inside that coal shed during the years before the cellar was boarded out. So many memories have been locked away safe in the box they have lain in for nearly thirty *years. I cannot bear to open that box now and it will serve no purpose to do so.*

Thrusting my hands inside the pockets of my coarse woolen jacket that is the colour of the night before me, I steel myself against the unwanted memories, shaking them from my mind as a wet dog would rid itself of the uncomfortable sensation of water on its coat. I am tired of this life that I have been given, that I have been forced to endure. It is time for me to move on, onwards towards my next destination. I prepared myself for death so long ago that it has just become a part of my psyche and barely requires even the most fleeting moment of recognition. But for once, I allow myself a brief foray of reflection, not of my life, for that ended when I was a child and learnt that there was more than one type of love. Instead, my thoughts lie with how my life might have been, if I had been like the other children at school who had been allowed to feel happiness and were shown the true meaning of love, not the sadistic, twisted version that I was shown. These emotions of love and happiness, I neither understand nor recognise, but still, I feel a twinge deep in the pit of my stomach that they were not destined to be a part of my life. I know why it could not be so, I was told often enough as a child – it was because I did not deserve to be loved. Every ounce of darkness in my life has been because of the inherent evil within me. Every bad thing that has happened to me has all been my fault. I alone must shoulder the burden of responsibility for what happened in the dark cellar underneath grandfather's house; the place where my father hid in the shadows at the top of the wooden staircase and watched; where my mother hid in her bedroom, her hands tightly fastened across her ears so that she could not hear my screams. During those long, lonely hours in the cellar, I often wondered if mother's own tears had blocked out the sound of my sobbing; a temporary deafness that had prevented her from hearing my pleading for her to help me. She did not help me. No one helped me. She abandoned me to my grandfather's attentions and never once acknowledged the dark secret hidden deep within the core of our family. Family. The very word makes me spit onto the dirt beneath my feet, leaving a bitter taste behind that nothing can wash away.

As I walk softly over the threshold of the back yard and across the cobbled path for the last time, I look around at the neighbouring houses to see glimpses of their lives. To the right of me an infant is crying, to the left, raised voices tell me that the baby's parents cannot afford to feed their children, though the father has still been to the pub as it is Friday night and he believes that he is entitled to a few pints with his friends after such a hard week at work. Suddenly it is gone. That haunting feeling that I had felt only moments ago, that longing for the merest crumb of a normal life. How could I compare all that I have achieved during my lifetime with the pathetic lives of those minions who know no better than to continue to perpetuate the cycle of poverty and abuse that encompasses the world they were born into. I too was born into that world, but I know better. I know that I have a purpose to my life, to teach the world the lessons that I have learnt. And afterwards, I will be free from the memories that haunt my dreams and shackle me to my past; free from the box that I do not wish to unlock, hidden deep inside my mind, where it will stay until I am no longer on this earth.

As I reach the end of the path, I stop to stand under the streetlamp that bathes me in a bright yellow light. I turn to look back up the alleyway that is now encased in darkness – and at the uniform rows of houses standing either side of the black void. Involuntarily a smile flickers across my face. No, I am not like them and nor would I want to be. I am me and I have achieved what I set out to do. I have earnt my freedom, set right what has been wronged. Now it is time for the next part of my journey. It is time for me to finally meet the death I have both revered, desired and feared for so long.

CHAPTER TWENTY SIX

The front door closes with a sharp click that echoes through the hallway. I slump against the wall, sliding down it until I am crouched on the floor. I am paralysed by fear and indecision, not understanding the reasoning behind my actions but recognising that my intuition is shouting at me not to tell the police about Alex. Perhaps it is the fear that Alex could find out what I have done that keeps my silence, or from some mis-placed loyalty that still resides within me to shield the person who once protected me. Or perhaps it is the small flame that flickers deep inside me, that I should be the one to end this game; it is my responsibility to stop Alex, for it is I who brought Alex into this house.

For a moment I am back there, sitting on the bottom step of the stairs, waiting for the sound of a car pulling up outside the house, listening for the sharp click of a key turning in the once well-oiled latch, the creak of a wooden door brushing up against a white wooden frame that has swollen and bowed over time. My mother was so proud of her house, with its neat front yard, bordered by rows of daffodils that flowered underneath the bay window year after year; the ornate metal railing separating the two adjoining houses, that somehow escaped from being sequestered for the war effort; the beautiful stained-glass door that reminds me of a nearby church that I once visited. She was so proud that she, the runt of the family, who had not even had a bed to call her own as a child, actually owned her own house. The fact that she had only acquired one through marriage was of no consequence to her, it was hers and that was all that mattered. I wonder what mother would have thought of her little house now; the place where a vile, sadistic creature has been harbouring within its four walls.

My attention is drawn away from my thoughts and back to the hallway again. Something has changed, something is different. The house is silent. Something is missing amongst the usual sounds within the house. The clock has stopped. The clock never stops.

A cold sensation runs through my body. Involuntarily I shiver, causing the tiny hairs on my upper arms to stand up, warning me that there is something very wrong in this house. Cautiously I stand up, placing one foot in front of the other, again and again, until I am half-way across the hallway. I try to suppress the rising panic that is threatening to halt me in my tracks. No matter how afraid I am, I must find out why the clock has stopped.

I edge towards the doorway of the sitting room, trying to control my rapidly accelerating heart, which is pounding inside of its cage. But my body cannot hide the fear that I am trying to quell and it reveals itself through the sensation of warm liquid that trickles down the inside of my left thigh. I watch as the pale-yellow liquid dribbles down my ankle and across the top of my foot, then meanders downwards onto the tiled floor below, where it pools into the crevices that were once white, before the grouting between the tiles wore away into dust.

Ignoring the damp sensation of my sodden clothes,

I step over the golden liquid and push open the door to the sitting room. The room is in darkness, curtains drawn to shut out the world outside. Guardedly I peek around the door, my eyes searching into the dark corners, noting the familiar objects in the room; the bureau with its doors still open; the standard lamp standing tall in the corner as if surveying its domain; the high back chair near the fireplace. My eyes automatically seek out the clock in the centre of the mantelpiece. The clock that is no longer ticking.

I stare at the clock as if willing it to yield its secrets, but of course it does not. It just sits there staring back at me defiantly, as if accusing me of being the cause of its malfunction.

Suddenly a wave of nausea washes over me, accompanied by a feeling of light headedness. The need for water is now greater than my desire for answers. I retreat from the threshold, step over the drying puddle on the floor and creep down the hallway, that is still encased in its quiet darkness.

The door to the kitchen is closed. Hesitantly I push it open and flick on the light, then pause for a moment to allow my eyes to adjust to the brightness. On the opposite side of the room is a cupboard that holds glasses and mugs, set out uniformly, equidistant from each other. I pad across the cold floor and pull out a glass, then move across the room to the kitchen sink. Flicking on the tap, I wait for the stagnant water to be replaced by fresh from the mains supply underneath the road in front of my house. As I wait for the warm water to be replaced with cool, something in the corner of the room catches my eye.

Slowly I turn my head to see what it is that has caught my attention. There is something different in the room and for a split second I cannot decipher what it is, as if my mind does not wish to acknowledge it. Then it clicks, as if a switch has been pulled in my mind. My eyes flick towards the door that leads out into the garden. There is something on the floor that was not there before. Reluctantly my eyes are drawn to look at the unfamiliar object; a small navy blue roll bag is lying on the floor, pushed up against the outer wall of the house. Bile rises up into the back of my throat as my brain quickly computes what this must mean; Alex.

CHAPTER TWENTY SEVEN

'Hello Beth, you didn't really think that I would leave you, did you?'
I open my mouth to answer, but the words do not form. The sound of running water jolts me from the dreamlike state I have found myself in. I reach over and place the glass under the tap, filling the glass almost to the top. My hand shakes as I bring the cool liquid to my mouth and gulp down a few mouthfuls, the water cutting through the nausea that is rising up my throat from the pit of my stomach.
    'Have you been keeping up with the news?'
    I nod my head, an almost imperceptible action, but a movement all the same and one that will not go unnoticed. Alex will take pleasure in my discomfort.
    I place the glass of water onto the worktop, fat droplets spilling onto the work surface. Alex is drinking it all in, breathing in every second of the pain that I have felt over the last few days, using it to replenish a strength that has waned. I am unable to move, rooted to the floor like a tree whose withered appendages penetrate deep into the rich earth. But a tree is strong and so now am I. I will not allow Alex back into my life again.
    I reach across to switch off the tap, leaving a bitter silence to fall across the room in its wake. The only audible sound is from my laboured breathing,

which cuts through the atmosphere like a knife. Just like the knives in the drawer, only centimetres away from where I am standing.

'I know what you're thinking Beth. It won't work. You will never be rid of me.'

How is it that Alex can read the thoughts that have been forming in my mind? Closing my eyes, I focus on my breathing, noticing the cool air as it fills my lungs, the upwards expansion of my rib cage, the warm, stale air as it exits again.

'What's the plan Beth? How do you think that you will rid yourself of me?' The words portray a steadfast confidence, but perhaps with a little less certainty than before. Something has shifted. My continuing silence is no longer borne out of fear, but from strength of mind.

My breathing slows down again. I open my eyes, blinking against the artificial light form the strip light above my head. 'It is over Alex, surely you must know that.'

A snort of derision tells me that Alex will not go easily, but I also sense a weariness, a longing perhaps to escape from a world that has been so cruel. I can feel the torrid mess inside of Alex, the swirling vortex that has consumed the inner being for so long, is now ready to be released.

My fingers inch their way across the worktop, feeling the cool, silky material beneath them, and inch slowly onwards towards the drawer, fingertips brushing against the handle. I gently grasp it and silently pull open the drawer, just wide enough for my fingertips to delve inside and feel for the knife that is always there. My hand clasps onto something smooth and cold.

I feel certain that my actions have been noticed and that there must be a tinge of guilt visible on my face that will betray my actions. For a moment I can sense a deep pool of anger within Alex, then suddenly it is gone, replaced by such sadness that I can barely stand to acknowledge it.

'Yes, you are right Beth, it is over. It is time for me to leave this world and all the cruelty within it. You are strong now. You do not need me anymore.'

Instinctively I know that these words are true. Alex came into my life when I needed a protector, a teacher, someone to show me the way forward. But I do not need Alex now. It is over

CHAPTER TWENTY EIGHT

And so it is that I am here again, sitting on the bottom step of the staircase, waiting for the car that has just pulled up outside. I listen intently as the dark purr of the diesel engine stops, then the driver's door slams shut with a heavy clunk that echoes down the quiet street. There are no other movements outside. It is as if the world has stopped, as if they too are waiting for this moment to occur.

Heavy footsteps march up the concrete path to the front door. For a brief moment, I expect to hear a key turn in the lock, but of course it cannot be so. Alex has gone.

My heart pounds as I wait for the knock that I know will surely come. It does not take long, seconds at most. There it is. A firm rap on the door, accompanied by a shadow lurking behind the stained glass window. I sit, motionless, unable to move from the spot where I have been sitting for so long.

The rapping becomes louder, more insistent, but still, I do not move. Then the letterbox opens and instantly I recognise the dull tone of PC Martin's voice.

'Beth, I know you're in there, please open the door.'

His words sound distant, as if I am hearing them through a dense fog. Through the gaping hole left by the now open letterbox, I see a pair of lips moving, but

I do not know what they say. So, I stay still, sitting on the bottom step of the stairs, in the same place that I have always sat when I have waited to receive whatever it is that life chooses to bring me next.

The brass door handle turns and the door tentatively opens. I can hardly bear to look as the figure approaches, making placatory noises as if I am a child needing to be soothed. I have been expecting this. I open my mouth to tell him all about Alex, but no words come out.

'It's ok, you don't need to talk now,' PC Martin says gently.

I close my eyes as tears form under tired lids then well down my cheeks in rivulets. I am safe.

PART TWO

BETH

CHAPTER TWENTY NINE

It is still dark. I thrust out a hand to feel for the bedside light switch. My fingers make contact with a smooth metal cylinder, then they travel half way up it to locate the push button. The anticipatory silence is interjected by a click, then light floods the room, bathing me with relief that I am no longer alone in the darkness.

My floral pyjamas are drenched in sweat from the same nightmare that has haunted me night after night for the past five years. I push back the coarse blue blanket, allowing the chill air to quickly cool my temperature.

On the bedside table is a plastic tumbler of water that I leave out every night as a matter of habit. I reach out to pick it up, the familiarity of the sensation of the cool liquid slipping down my throat, soothes my frazzled mind. With most of the glass emptied of its contents, I return it to the table again, ensuring that the glass is in the centre of the placemat.

Next to the lamp there is a rectangular notepad, the blue pastel hardcover folded underneath, ready for use. A biro lies beside it, as yet unused. I pick it up, fingers still trembling a little from the horror of the night. Twisting the pen between my fingers, I stare at the blank page, which in turn stares back at me. I am supposed to write down my dreams, not only as a record of the workings of my inner mind, but to absolve myself of the heavy burden that awakens me night after night. But I do not yet feel ready to share the pain that is inside of me. Instead, I place the pad and pen back onto the table and chastise myself for my seemingly never-ending failings that are always there to disappoint me.

Taking a deep breath, I focus my attention on the room where I have slept for the last few months. I observe the contents as if seeing it for the first time; the oversized bay window with its old-fashioned radiator beneath the peeling windowsill; the thin grey carpet that provides me with little relief from the cold floorboards beneath, even when I am wearing the slippers that one of the staff gave to me last Christmas.

Swinging my legs over the side of the bed, I place my feet onto the threadbare carpet, feeling the coarse fibres on the underside of my toes. I pad softly across the room, mindful that the other residents could still be sleeping at this early hour. Drawing back the thin curtains in one confident movement, reveals that the day has already begun to dawn. The oak tree that frames the view from my room has begun to spring into life following the barren winter months. The leaves once fully formed, will provide adequate protection from predators for the blackbirds and sparrows who will soon be nesting within its thick branches. In the distance, smoke lazily climbs from chimneys in the nearby village, from fires that would have been lit the previous night to ward off the chill evening air. I gaze at the shadow of the rooflines against the failing moonlight, trying to ascertain where the tea-room is located - where one day I hope that I will be allowed to visit. As soon as I am well enough. The other residents have told me that the tea-room is in the central shopping street and offers the most magnificent oversized scones, laden with strawberry jam and clotted cream, that can be washed down with a huge teapot of strong tea that always ends up a little stewed by the time the scone has been consumed. It is the type of place where finger sandwiches are served, and more than one type of coffee is available to attend to all their customers' needs. It is odd to think how something that most people would consider normal, mundane even, fills my heart with such joy and spurs me on to continue to work towards my goals.

I turn away from the window and survey the rest of the room. In the far corner is a pine wardrobe, and next to it, is a small handbasin, where I can wash and refill my glass of water during the night. I barely notice the quietness anymore. I have grown used to the absence of the clock now, though I still hear it in my dreams. Tick, tick, tick, that endless measure of time, the constant reminder of the past. There are no clocks in my little room at the top of the Victorian building that I now call my home. For the first time in my life, I truly feel safe. I am comforted by the routine, the regularity of meal times and medication schedules, the surety of knowing when it is time to go to bed and when to wake up again. The predictability of nature is also a comfort for me; the dawn chorus tells me that I am still alive; the nesting birds in the spring remind me that life continues regardless of what has passed and the autumn leaf fall heralds the cold bitter winds that will surely follow. I cannot remember a time when I have felt so at peace, both with life and within myself.

I still recall the blanket of peace that descended upon me, that day at my mother's house when the police came for me. It was as if somehow I knew that the nightmare I had endured for so long was now over and all would be well again with the world. Not long after that day, my mother's beloved home was sold for a pitiful price, its value diminished greatly by Alex's actions. It was not possible for me to stay there any longer and even if it were, I could not bear to live any longer in the mausoleum that I had created.

My thoughts are interrupted by a gentle knocking at the door. The handle slowly turns and a grey-haired head peeks around the door. 'Good morning Beth, how are you today?'

'I'm very well, thank you Sylvie.'

A beaming smile breaks out across Sylvie's plump face. Words cannot express the joy I feel at seeing her friendly, warm face every morning. I still find it hard to believe how much my life has changed. It has been a difficult journey that is not yet over, but I have already come a long way and am immeasurably grateful for all those who are accompanying me on this voyage. Even after five years, it still feels alien to me that anyone would seemingly take delight in seeing me, let alone for them to ask me how I am feeling with the expectation of receiving a genuine response, rather than the usual polite platitudes that society has taught us to express. Even stranger, is having the opportunity to express my feelings, something that I am still finding hard. But I am making progress, and I know this, as I am told so frequently.

'Here you go Beth,' Sylvie says as she administers three tablets into a plastic cup and hands it to me. She watches unashamedly as I pour the tablets into my mouth and swill them down with the small measure of water that she placed on the top of the chest of drawers. I know that she is watching to ensure I swallow the tablets, seeing them move down my throat to the point of no return. I do not mind, she only wants to keep me well and prevent me from returning to the pit of fire that I was living in before I came to this place.

Sylvie replaces the two empty paper cups onto the trolley that she has left in the hallway; a metal framed chariot poised expectantly on top of the faded carpet runner, awaiting its next destination. 'I shall leave you to get dressed Beth. Breakfast will be in twenty minutes. I'll see you downstairs then.'

I smile in response, then turn my attention to finding something to wear. I open the door to the wardrobe and observe the line of clothes hanging neatly in the wardrobe, all in order of graduated colours, starting from the lightest on the left to the darkest on the right-hand side.

'Welcome Beth, please sit down,' Dr Hastings says warmly, pointing to an unoccupied chair. Twelve pairs of eyes follow me as I walk through the circle to take up the vacant seat. Dr Hastings smiles reassuringly at me, as if she understands the discomfort that I am currently feeling. I have never liked to be the centre of attention and I am aware that my infamy is well known here amongst the other residents. Still, it has taken a long time to get to this point - where I have been deemed well enough to participate in group therapy and I must push my social awkwardness to one side. This moment marks the start of my recovery, the rebuilding of a life into something worth living. However self-conscious I feel right now, I must relish this opportunity with vigour, for it is a complete contrast to the turgid passivity to which I have become accustomed.

This is not just a group session though, where everyone talks about their feelings. It is one where the very reason for their arrival at this place is acknowledged, accepted and put into the past. For some, this stage will never come, for others, they will become stuck and stagnate, unable to acknowledge what has occurred in their lives, or unwilling to draw a line underneath it to leave it behind. Dr Hastings has already warned me of the difficulties that I will face with this task. For it is not possible for me to entirely leave my past behind, but instead I must place it in a box and store it, where hopefully it will remain. I know that I am different from the others, that I am an oddity, a circus of curiosity that has piqued the interest of everyone within this establishment. But I do not want to be a side show anymore. I long for a normal existence and will do anything to make it happen.

'Thank you everyone for joining today's meeting. I am pleased to see that everyone has turned up. Please take a moment to welcome Beth to the group.' Dr Hastings pauses for a moment, her eyes moving to each person in turn, waiting expectantly for some acknowledgement of what she has just said.

I too am watching the group carefully and count three people who have smiled in response to Dr Hastings' words, and eight stony faces who could not have made it any more obvious that they do not want me here. I will not allow it to bother me though, I have never had friends and have no expectations of making any, despite the enjoyment I have experienced from the friendly demeanor of the staff. I am here for the specific purpose of beginning the journey that will eventually lead to my release from here and I am determined that I will get through this process, with or without the help of my fellow residents.

'Beth, perhaps we can start with you today?'

'I'm not sure what to say?' I say, plucking at a loose thread on the seam of my jeans.

'Well, how about how you ended up here?'

'I don't know where to start.'

The thin smile begins to waver. 'Ok, I think perhaps this is too hard for you today, shall we hear from one of the others and we can come back to your story next time?'

I nod, grateful to put off the inevitable for another time. I know that the rest of the group are eager to hear my story, but it is not one that I am yet ready to tell.

The session lasts for over an hour, but I cannot say what was said. I was too busy concentrating on a spider that was crawling up the wall opposite me, to take notice of the words coming out of a stranger's mouth. I have no interest in what they have to say in any case.

Suddenly the session ends. The residents who are sitting opposite, push back their chairs and file out of the room first, swiftly followed by those sitting either side of me. Slowly I stand up to follow, unsure of where I should be going next. I am unused to this level of freedom and look to Dr Hastings for instructions.

A gentle hand appears on my shoulder, 'Beth, I think it would help if you write down your story, that way you can just read it out at our next group session.'

I smile, the response I always give when I do not know how I am supposed to react. Even though I have been here now for five years, I am still uncertain of my part in this strange game.

The rest of the group have all by now disappeared out of sight. Dr Hastings notices the look of concern on my face, that I have been left behind. 'Why don't you go and catch them up Beth.'

I smile again at Dr Hastings, a little more warmly

than before, then stride at pace down the stark, colourless corridor.

The other residents have gathered in the small common room, where a hot water urn sits on a teak table near the bay window, ready for anyone who wishes to make themselves a mug of tea. I glance in through the doorway at the group, who seemingly have not noticed my absence, then continue down the corridor towards the door that leads to the garden.

The fragile winter sun is low in the sky, but even so, it is strong enough to warm my face and lift my spirits a little. I walk towards a sycamore tree, underneath which a blackbird is sitting, pulling at a worm that emerged during last night's rainstorm. Nestled amongst the leaves on the lowest branch of the tree, a sparrow huddles, trying to shelter from the biting wind that is beginning to strengthen. I watch as the yellow and brown leaves that fell the previous autumn, are picked up by the breeze. They swirl around in circles, close to the blackbird, who has now given up trying to extract the worm from the dense soil.

The concrete path takes me around the gigantic tree and onwards to the perimeter wall; a steadfast, red-brick structure that curls protectively around the estate. Beyond the wall is the village with the pretty tea-room that shuts during the winter months. I know what it is that I must do in order to elicit a visit to the tea-room, but can I bring myself to accept who Alex really is, and more importantly, what Alex has done? If I am ever going to be released though, this is what I will need to do.

My head begins to pound, as it always does, when I think of Alex. I turn around to head back up the path towards the back door, which has been left propped open, even though it was drummed into us on our first day, that fire doors should never be left ajar.

There is no one else out in the garden today, for although it is sunny, it is bitterly cold. As if reading my thoughts, the wind whistles along the path, bringing with it a gust of cold air and a flurry of withered leaves, some of which have lost colour, their transparency bringing yet another reminder of death.

Pulling the sleeves of my jumper down over my hands to shield them from the biting chill, I clasp onto the antique brass handle and pull the heavy outer door open a little further so that I can step inside. Immediately my shoes sink into the deep-pile carpet, a sharp contrast to the hardness of the concrete path that I have just been walking on. Even though I am now inside the building, I can still feel the chilly air on my back. I quicken my step so that I am out of its reach and quickly traverse the length of the hallway. At the end of the corridor, the door to the TV room is open. From inside, I can hear laughter from the other residents who are watching a sit-com. Even though I am now allowed to join them, I seldom do so, preferring instead my own company, tucked away from the prying eyes and probing stares. They all know who I am and why I am here. Unlike the other residents, it seems that I am not allowed to forget my past.

I stand at the threshold and peer inside. I cannot imagine ever sitting on one of the grey, plastic chairs, cackling with laughter at some figure on the TV who believes that falling over is an adequate form of entertainment. I do not fit in here, just as I have never fitted in anywhere. It is time for me to find a way to leave this place, so that I can live a life away from those prying eyes and probing questions, always wanting to know how I am, how I feel. Always wanting to know about Alex.

CHAPTER THIRTY

As I push open the heavy fire-resistant door, with its lead-lined glass panels that I have been assured are unbreakable, every person in the room turns around to stare. I know that I should be used to this by now, but I am not. I seem to be unable to harden myself to this unwanted attention, no matter how hard I try. Perhaps this is the reason for Alex appearing in my life; to protect me from those who mistreat me.

I pull out the only unoccupied chair in the circle. The grating noise from the metal feet scraping across the parquet floor, cuts through the anticipatory atmosphere. I take off my woolen blue cardigan and place it on the back of the chair, which creaks ominously under my slight frame. I sit down with intense trepidation for what is about to occur.

I do not need to look up to know that my every move is being watched. I can sense it. The prying eyes are waiting for me to share my story, to explain myself to them, so that they can understand all that I am unable to. I know that to leave this place, I cannot put off this process any longer. My desire for freedom, is greater than the fear I hold within to acknowledge the past and accept myself for the person that I am. I must be strong. Like Alex.

'Thank you for joining us, Beth,' Dr Hastings begins, her ever-present smile wavering a little under my steady gaze. She catches herself and the smile reappears more firmly, perhaps a little more falsely than before. 'Perhaps today we can hear from you?'

My nod is almost imperceptible, but it is an affirmation all the same. There is an air of thick tension across the room, an excited anticipation of the session that is about to begin.

'I'm sure all those who have joined this morning's session would like to give Beth their encouragement. This is the first time Beth has chosen to speak and I'm sure everyone remembers how difficult that can be.'

I glance around the room, noting smiles of encouragement from some of the group, along with looks of curiosity from the others.

'I should not need to remind you all, that everything said here is confidential and must not be taken outside of the room.' Murmurs of agreement reassure Dr Hastings that the point has been duly noted. She turns to look at me, the smile still firmly in place.

'Well then Beth, perhaps you would like to tell the group a little about Alex?'

I take a deep breath and release the carbonised air again in a steady flow, my racing pulse quietening a little with the action. 'Alex first appeared in my life when I was five years old,' I began.

'Was there a reason for Alex appearing at that time? Did something happen to you when you were five?'

'My brother died. He walked out into the North Sea when we were on holiday on the Suffolk coast. I never saw him alive again.'

'How did you feel when your brother died?'

'Shocked, lonely, angry that he had left me. He had always protected me, you see.' I look to see if Dr Hastings realises the importance of what I have just said.

Dr Hastings nods, then motions for me to continue.

'Not long after my brother died, I was sent to stay with my grandparents.'

'Why was that, Beth?'

'Mother couldn't cope, you see. She couldn't look after a small child, she wasn't capable of it. Her grief seemed to be endless, she was a ghost of the person she once was.' I look around the room to see if the group are still listening and find fixed gazes upon me, not this time with looks of curiosity, but through the recognition of shared life experience.

'It was not just the grief of losing her first born child that turned my mother into an empty shell, it was also the truth that she could not admit to herself; that she had failed to keep her child safe from harm. She failed to keep my brother from walking out into the sea to his death.' I look up to see several heads nod in acknowledgment of my words. Suddenly I am curious to know the other residents' stories, if they too have had similar experiences to me.

'How did you feel about being sent to stay with your grandparents?'

'Afraid and very alone.'

'Is that when Alex appeared in your life?'

'Yes. I had been living with grandma and grandad for three weeks when Alex first came into my life. Alex was my protector.'

'What was it that Alex needed to protect you from Beth?'

I stand up, as if the trance that I have been held in, has suddenly vanished. 'I don't want to talk anymore today.'

'You've done very well Beth. Please can everyone thank Beth for sharing some of her story today.' The tense quietness of the room is replaced by quiet clapping and murmurs of gratitude that I have found the courage at last to speak up.

'Thank you everyone, this morning's session is now over. Please take your jumpers and cardigans and make your way to the dining room for lunch.'

Dr Hastings holds open the door to allow everyone out of the room, one by one into the corridor beyond. As always, I am the last to leave, traipsing behind the group like an unwanted puppy.

As I pass through the doorway, Dr Hastings places a hand onto my right arm and squeezes it firmly. 'Well done for today, Beth. It's very hard to do what you did, be proud of your progress.'

I manage a sliver of a smile in response, then hurry down the windowless corridor, anxious to put the morning behind me.

It is the same routine every day at Brackenfield House. Even the choice of lunch menu has a routine. Apparently, it helps to orientate the residents to know which day of the week it is when they know what to expect to be eating. I'm sure there is some logic behind it, for it can be disorientating when there is so little variation to the day. Today is Thursday, which means there will be a roast dinner, often chicken, but sometimes beef, followed by a stodgy steamed pudding with custard. After lunch there is an hour of free time, where we can wander through the grounds, or play cards in the common room with some of the other residents. We are called residents to give us a sense of identity, though the metal bars across the downstairs window leave us in no doubt that we are not here voluntarily.

The ethos of Brackenfield is to rehabilitate and only those who are judged as having some possibility of release are sent here. From my five years' experience of residency here though, it seems few residents are actually rehabilitated to the extent that they are no longer a danger to themselves or to society. Many of the residents were puzzled by my arrival given the circumstances, but still, here I am, sitting on a bench in the gardens at the rear of the enormous Victorian house, pondering whether I will ever be able to walk through the vast iron gates at the far end of the grounds.

The freedom to walk alone through the grounds is a privilege that I have earnt through hard work and diligence; taking my meds consistently every morning and every evening and portraying a willingness to talk about my life. At first those conversations were restricted between myself and Dr Hastings, but the programme dictates that the patient needs to be accepted by others for what they have done, and so requires them to share their inner thoughts and feelings with the other residents in their assigned group.

Behind the wooden bench on which I am sitting, purple crocuses are starting to emerge in the flowerbed underneath the large bay window of the group therapy room that I was in earlier. Spring flowers have always represented hope for me, a reminder of the emergence from the winter that has been left behind. The vision of the delicate flowers reminds me of the flower bed in the front garden of my mother's house and of the time that I watched her kneeling in the soft, grainy earth, planting daffodil bulbs in the autumn, so that they would emerge in the spring. I wonder if they are still there.

'Beth! It's time to come in now,' Sylvie calls from the doorway. She is standing just inside the half open door, trying to shelter from the bitter wind that is blowing up the garden towards the house.

I shiver, as if only now noticing the cold for the first

time. Gingerly I stand up and wait patiently for the numbness in my knees to subside. As soon as the feeling has returned to my limbs, I make my way back up the path. Sylvie smiles at me as I brush past her ample figure to pass through the gap that has been created by her holding the door open for me. The initial feeling of relief that I am out of the bitter cold, is quickly replaced by disappointment that I am back in the windowless corridor, back to the life that I escaped from in my mind only moments ago.

Most of the other residents are already in their bedrooms, having some quiet time before supper. After a simple meal of hot soup and toasted sandwiches, it will be bath time. There is a bath rota, so that there are no arguments over whose turn it is, as if we are children who need to be reminded how to behave like civilised adults. Unlike some residents, I do not mind the rules. They make me feel safe for the first time in my life, though of course I still long to have control over my own life. Perhaps one day I will.

Later on in the evening, there will be warm milk and biscuits, which we can take to our bedrooms, where we can read quietly, or write letters to our families - if we have reached the level where we have been granted permission to communicate with the outside world. I have not got to that level yet, but it is not one that I have any desire to reach, for I have no one to write to.

Bedtimes are always the same, no matter if it is a week day or the weekend, when there are no therapy sessions and some of the more privileged residents on higher levels are allowed contact sessions with their families. Sylvie always appears as if by magic at nine o'clock prompt, with the medicine trolley in tow. I have often wondered how it is that she is with us every day, but of course I would not ask such a personal question. I do have a theory though that perhaps she was once a resident and chose not to leave the safety of the institution for the unknown world outside. Perhaps one day I will ask.

Lights must always be out at ten o'clock. Sometimes when I am not feeling tired enough to sleep, I sit curled up on the deep windowsill and look out at the dark shapes in the garden, trying to work out what they are. In the distance, the lights from the nearby village illuminate the darkness. They remind me of the fairy lights that my mother used to fastidiously place around the dark green fronds of a potted fir tree, that was always in front of the open fire in the living room on Christmas Eve. When I gaze out of the window at the lights, I often wonder about the people who live in the village and the lives that they lead. One day soon, I promise myself, I will go there.

CHAPTER THIRTY ONE

Several weeks pass before I feel up to talking again at the group session. It is as if I have been encased in a black fog that has shielded me from my emotions, unable to communicate with the world and rendering me unknowing of the passing of time. The efforts of both Sylvie and Dr Hastings to reach wherever it is that my mind has drifted off to, go unrivalled, with even the presence of a cream tea from the village tea room brought up to my bedroom, remaining unnoticed. Instead, it was the sight of the baby blackbirds nesting in the sycamore tree outside my bedroom window and the reminder of new beginnings that began to penetrate through the dense fug. And later, it was the warmth of the summer sun that gradually lifted the confounding haze, thawing the numbness that blanketed me and allowing me to think coherently one again.

Newly awoken from my strange slumber, the thought of baring my soul to a room of strangers after the solitude of the last few weeks, sickens me to the pit of my stomach. But not as much as the growing impatience inside of me, that shouts to find a way out of here and into a different life. My initial enthusiasm at this game we are being forced to play is starting to wane, and so I need to steel myself against my feelings and focus only on what needs to be done.

'Beth, would you like to talk to us more about Alex today?'

'Yes, ok,' I reply unenthusiastically. I take a deep breath as I gather my thoughts to decide where to begin. 'As I've said before, Alex was my protector. So, when grandfather died and I no longer needed protecting, Alex left my life again. I did not imagine that Alex would ever return.'

'When did Alex return?'

'It was not long after mother died. My father had died several years before then and we had got on quite happily with our lives in that time. I looked after mother, did her shopping and cleaning and in the evenings, we would watch the local news followed by soaps on TV. Her favourite was Emmerdale Farm. I preferred Coronation Street, but it was her TV of course, so she chose what we watched.'

Dr Hastings nodded empathetically. 'Why do you think it was then that Alex came back into your life?'

'I've always hated being on my own. I was lost after mother died. I had no purpose anymore.'

'What happened Beth, when Alex returned?'

'At first, I was happy that I was no longer alone. I didn't feel scared anymore, I had Alex to look after me, to be my companion.'

'Go on', Dr Hastings says encouragingly.

'I don't know when it started, or how, but Alex wanted to be in control of me. Suddenly Beth wasn't good enough, couldn't do anything right. Beth was weak and useless.'

A murmur of sympathy was heard across the room. There were many others in the group who knew how that felt.

'What happened next Beth,' Dr Hastings says softly, placing a hand gently onto my forearm and squeezing it a little.

'Alex became angry, unpredictable. It was as if a dam had been opened and the river behind it unleashed. All that anger just flooded out like a torrent to wreak its revenge on all that lay in its path.'

'What would happen when Alex was angry?'

'Alex didn't want revenge if that's what you're thinking. It wasn't like that.'

'What was it like then Beth?'

'Alex found a way to set us free.'

'And did Alex's actions set you both free?'

'No, they didn't and poor Beth has been left to pick up the broken pieces and glue them back together again.'

'Thank you, Beth,' Dr Hastings says, removing her hand from my arm. 'I think that will be enough for today.'

I stare at Dr Hastings, wanting to ask the question that I dare not ask. Has the river been contained? Has Alex been contained? And if so, does this mean that one day Beth might get to see the daughter she loves so very much but has not yet held?.

CHAPTER THIRTY TWO

And so, here I sit, on a small metal chair, pen and paper in front of me, waiting patiently for my story to begin. I have so much to say, I hardy know where to start. Perhaps I should begin with the dream that endlessly haunts my slumber, the one where child after child is led by the hand down the rickety wooden stairs into the cold, dark cellar, never to return.

The images that came so easily to mind of the children in the cellar, vanishes, and is replaced by the vision of a blue fountain pen, lying askew in the centre of the crisp, white sheet. I stare at the piece of paper in front of me as it grounds me to the present moment, then focus my mind back onto the task ahead. Despite the cocktail of drugs that I am coerced to take, my mind has gained some clarity for the first time in a very long time. It is as if the once impenetrable fog has begun to clear, the dark images hiding in the background are beginning to emerge from a ghostly mist and take the form of something familiar in the light. But the fog has not yet full dissipated and the sinister dark shadows that have been hidden away for so long, still linger in the depths of my mind.

I have learnt much about myself through my conversations with Dr Hastings. I know that my mind has been very clever and locked away the painful memories from my childhood to protect me. But now it is time for the box to be opened and for recollections that I have no desire to remember, to be released.

An image comes to mind, of a small child, sitting on the bottom step of the stairs, hands laced together in front of her knees. She tugs at the burgundy corduroy pinafore dress she is wearing, trying to make the thick material stretch a little further down over her cold knees. She is waiting, waiting for a car to pull up at the road in front of her little house. To her right, a couple stand motionless on the tiled floor in the hallway, two dark brown leather suitcases resting at their feet.

'It won't be for long,' father says, with a promise that the child instinctively knows is a lie. 'It's just until your mother has had a rest and is feeling better.'

The small child looks up at her mother, who is staring at the front door without seeing what is in front of her.

'We'll stay for one night Beth, but then I'll need to take mother to the rest home. You'll be ok with grandma and grandad, they'll look after you. You'll hardly notice we're not there.'

I look at my father and stare into the deep brown eyes that cannot meet my gaze. A yellow light flashes through the stained-glass window that comprises the top half of the wooden front door. Somewhere in the distance, a car door slams shut, the sound reverberating in the mist that is creeping up the road. Measured footsteps clip up the front path, then a dark shadow appears on the other side of the door. He is here.

I think back to that day on the beach. I was five years old, playing happily in the sand, building sandcastles and decorating them with the tiny shells I had found the previous day amongst the rocks. I did not notice my brother walking out into the sea. He was only ten years old. What must he have endured to want to die when he had not yet had the chance to live his life.

Another image comes to mind, of another young girl, sitting on the stony sand, watching as her dog runs into the sea to retrieve a ball. I can almost hear the sound of the waves forcefully crashing onto the shingle beach; breathe in the sharp salty air that pours into all of your senses, filling them with innocent pleasure that cleanses your mind. The child, wind tussling her shoulder-length hair, is running along the sand, the little brown mongrel at her side. She looks so much like her father, the same chestnut brown hair with a slight curl, that wide toothy grin. The same care-free laugh as she throws the ball across the beach. It lands heavily into the sea, sending foamy sea spray high up into the air before it drops back into the grey waves again. The dog looks at the girl for a moment as if to say, 'Shall I?' then leaps into the air, crashing into the waves. Seconds later the dog returns to the beach, the ball firmly gripped between his jaws.

My mother came from a small seaside town, the type where everyone knew each other and looked after each other. A place where people had few material belongings but knew how to care for their neighbours. I still recall the cottage we went to every summer, the two-up-two-down stone built terraced house built for the fishermen who once lived in the village and made their livelihoods from the North Sea. It is there that I wish for my child to be raised and have the care-free childhood I had always wanted. And when she is older, I will tell her the truth - that one day her father knocked on my front door to sell me double glazing that I did not need and that I had felt so utterly alone since my mother's death, that I had invited him in for a cup of tea so that the silence of the house could be broken for a short while.

It was only through my sessions with Dr Hastings that I learnt that it had been the salesman who had forced open the weak lock on the back door and found his way up to my bedroom. I never saw him again after that night in the shed, when he came back to carry out his depraved longings and nearly rid me of our child.

I shake the image away again and it is replaced by one of Alex. Alex my protector. Dr Hastings has explained to me why Alex came into my life, to protect Beth from enduring the horror of what was occurring at 6 Ivry Street.

My mind wanders to the pile of documents lying on the desk. On the top of the pile is a folded newspaper that is yellowing with age. Carefully I unfold it and smooth out the wrinkled pages.

I refold the piece of paper and place it gently back onto the table. I pick up another one and gingerly unfold it. Placing it flat on the table, I smooth out the pages, then squint to read the faded words that are written across the centre of the front page. It is a Last Will and Testament, the one that I found under the floorboards in the room that was once my brother's. A Will that was drawn up when I was just six years old, the year after my brother died. I still recall the sight of his lifeless body; his colourless face had been smashed against the rocks by the cruel sea rendering him almost unrecognisable. By the time a local fisherman had pulled him out of the water, it was difficult to tell this creature had once been my beloved brother; the person who had protected me from the evil that resided within the four walls of a two-up, two-down terraced house in Ivry Street. Until that is, the day came when he could no longer endure the evil being enacted upon him.

I am a small child again, standing behind my bedroom door clutching a yellow teddy bear in a tiny hand. I have been awoken from a deep, peaceful slumber by the sound of footsteps creaking across the landing floorboards, the sound of a boy sobbing as he is led down the stairs, along the hallway, and in through the cellar door. I am a curious child and cannot stop myself from opening the bedroom door, just the tiniest chink, needing to understand what is happening in the tense quietness of 6 Ivry Street. I am not the only one watching, my father is standing in the doorway to his bedroom. Behind him, my mother is sitting on the bed, eyes shut, hands clasped over her ears. My father does not see the eyes of a small child peering into the dimly lit landing as he gently closes the bedroom door. The quiet void is immediately replaced by music from the radio that sits on my parents' bedside table, filling the air with the most beautiful sound that I have ever heard.

It was not that night that I understood what was happening in my grandparents' house. It was only when my brother walked out into the cold North Atlantic sea, never to return and it was my turn to be led by the hand into that cold, dark cellar, that my curiosity was finally satiated.

The sound of paper dropping to the floor brings me back to the present day. I am back in my bedroom again, sitting behind the desk that overlooks the hospital grounds. My eyes drink in the familiar sight; the imposing tree in front of the sash window; the lights from the village that now seem a lifetime away. The familiarity of it all comforts me and my breathing starts to slow down again to a resting pace. I am safe.

I stoop down to pick up the Last Will and Testament of Stanley Charles Bonner, which has fallen from my grasp. I pick it up and place it back onto the table, automatically smoothing out the pages. Turning over the front page, I slowly read through the document line by line, just as I have done so many times, until I reach the section that I am looking for;

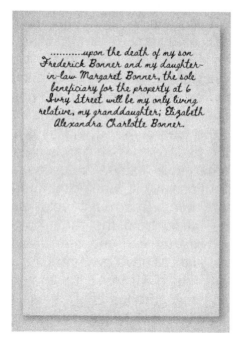

...upon the death of my son Frederick Bonner and my daughter-in-law Margaret Bonner, the sole beneficiary for the property at 6 Ivory Street will be my only living relative, my granddaughter; Elizabeth Alexandra Charlotte Bonner.

Putting the document back onto the desk again, I pick up a pen and place the nib at the top of the page. My hand shakes a little from the side-effects of the drugs that I take every morning when I awaken and every evening just before bedtime; the drugs that I have been told will keep Alex locked away in a box in my mind.

I press the pen gently down onto the paper and the words I have been so hesitant to speak, begin to flow onto the page. Hours pass in a trance-like state, barely acknowledging the knock on the door with my breakfast, which remains untouched. Nor do I hear the five-minute warning that the group session is about to start. It is only the arrival of Dr Hastings at my side that draws me momentarily from the task.

'Beth, we were worried about you, but I can see that you are busy so I will leave you in peace,' Dr Hastings smiles warmly, a flash of pride in her eyes that her hard work is paying off. At last, her most challenging patient is working to reveal the secrets she holds deep within.

By the time I have told my story and released the demons of my past, the day has passed and night has fallen. Through the window, I can see the occasional star before it is once more obscured by thick cloud that is threatening to unleash its burden over Brackenfield House. I place the pen down next to the thick wad of paper in the centre of the pine desk, then push back the chair to stand and stretch my aching back, like a cat who has spent the day in a long, peaceful slumber. For a moment, I allow my eyes to drink in the night sky, captivated by the blood moon whose orange light fills my soul. The shadows of the darkness have now dissipated, leaving only a quiet recognition that the past is now behind me. It is time for me to move on.

I step away from the window and pull the curtains across, then focus my attention back to the room that has become my sanctuary. Automatically I am drawn to the wad of paper on the desk that was once blank, but is now filled. The upper most sheet of paper contains only one sentence, it is the title that I have given to the story of my life:

"Fractured Mind" by Beth and Alex Bonner.

PART THREE

CHARLIE

CHAPTER THIRTY THREE

There is something that is bothering me; a niggling feeling that something is not quite right. It was at one of the group sessions that the feeling first arose, when I was alerted to the possibility that there is something else, hidden deep within my mind, something that has not yet come to light. It was the occasion when I first spoke in front of the group, the first time I spoke openly about Alex to someone other than Dr Hastings.

It had taken a long time to get to that point, where I was able to accept Alex and to acknowledge the truth of Alex's existence. I had been with Dr Hastings for four years when I learnt the truth about Alex.

'Beth, do you realise that Alex only exists in your mind?'

'What do you mean? I don't understand?'

'Well, sometimes when a child has gone through the sort of trauma that you went through, the mind can be very clever and to protect itself, it creates another personality.'

'But how could that be? I have heard Alex's voice. We have had conversations.'

'Yes, that's possible. Sometimes people who have more than one personality do not know about the other ones, and sometimes they do know about the others. They can also talk to each other, whether they are fully aware of the other voices or not.'

'But Alex was in my house. I heard the front door opening, footsteps up the stairs, the bath being run.'

'The noises were from your neighbours. It was the sounds from their everyday lives that had filtered through the thin adjoining wall that separated your worlds.'

Silence descended whilst I digested this information. It was something that seemed to make sense to me, and yet I still did not understand it. 'What about the cupboard? The punishments? Ivry Street.'

'I realise this is very hard for you Beth, but it is possible for the other voices to make the person do things that they would not normally do.'

'So, are you saying that it was me who took those girls?'

'No, it was Alex. It is important for you to understand that. It was not you Beth, it was Alex who did all those things. That's why it is so important for you to take your meds. Alex needs to be kept locked up.'

Since that day though there has been something else playing on my mind. It has been as if the dots are not quite connecting sufficiently well enough to reveal the picture hidden within. The words that I spoke at the first group session also keep coming back to me. They churn over and over again in my mind, and although I recognise their significance, it is not until now that I have understood why.

For when I spoke of Alex, coming into my life as my protector, I spoke the truth, for that is all Alex has ever been, no matter how it has appeared to the outside world. Everything Alex has done has been to protect me, not just from the world I have existed in and the terror that I have endured, but from myself. It is not Alex that the world needs to fear.

I have not told anyone of my suspicions, not even my beloved Dr Hastings, whom I trust more implicitly than any other human being in this world. And here lies the dilemma, for there is something that still haunts my dreams, night after night, something that I fear the burden of, will push me back into the dark abyss again. If I unburden myself and reveal my secret, I may very well obtain the absolution I crave so deeply, but I may also seal my fate and never be released from Brackenfield. For the only possibility of that occurring, will be if Alex, who has been blamed for all of this mess, is contained in such a way as to never be released.

The alternative is to stay silent and hope that I can contain the secret I hold deep within and somehow resolve this dissonance within me. There is however an even greater fear that I have than my own absolution. For this is a creature who is all of our nightmares and more; an entity so evil that I fear to even acknowledge its existence. For it is one that I fear will never be contained, but will bend others to do its will, just as it has done with Alex. Just as I fear that it will do with Beth.

The long summer days pass with little acknowledgment, for time is of no importance when one's mind is in such disarray. I wrestle with my conscience, with the voices in my head whose conflicting arguments cause such utter exhaustion, that I barely register the outside world. Even the presence of Dr Hastings does nothing to soothe me, and her confusion over the sudden reversal in my progress, haunts me. I simply do not know what to do and the indecision is tearing my soul apart. Is Beth strong enough to contain the other voice within her? For if she is not than the consequences will be dire. And what of poor Alex, who has been blamed for all that has happened? Alex has been separated from Beth, making her feel very alone and scared. For Alex is Beth's only true friend, the only one she can rely upon, the only one she can talk to and trust. Can Beth be strong enough without Alex's help? Can she trust herself not to let the other voice manipulate her, just as Alex has been used? Poor Alex believed that everything had to be done to set Beth free, but it was all lies.

And now the other voice wants Beth to maintain her silence, so that she can appear to recover and escape from these walls. The voice wishes to be free again, to carry on with the lessons it was taught so succinctly as a child.

One morning I wake up a little later than usual, to find the first rays of the low winter sun rising above the sycamore tree outside my window. I lie in bed and listen to the blackbirds, who are vigorously celebrating the new day. For the first time in months, a sense of calm prevails over me. It is as if a dark cloud has been lifted from my mind and now I can clearly see the path that I need to choose. The battle is over. The decision has been made.

The floor below my naked feet is cold as I creep across the room towards my desk. Lying on top of the worn desk, is the thick wad of paper containing the account of my life, that I wrote in early spring. I pull out the chair and sit down, noting the comforting familiarity of the hard seat moulding into my back, my bare feet automatically finding their usual spot underneath the desk. Pulling the manuscript towards me, I stare at the front page for a moment, then read the title over and over again. A smile forms at the surety of what I am about to do. Picking up a pencil, I place the tip onto the page just after Alex's name and in ghost like precision, I etch a name onto the page with such lightness that none other than myself will know it is there; "*Charlie*".

ABOUT THE AUTHOR

J. D. Missen was born and raised in a small seaside town in Suffolk - the type of place that is overrun with tourists in the summer months and in the winter, an anticipatory quiet descends. She was first inspired to write after studying First World War poetry at school and had poetry published in several anthologies. This passion for writing soon developed into writing fiction and quickly settled into the crime fiction and psychological thriller genres though she also has an interest in history, particularly modern and local history. J.D. Missen has also written two childrens books; 'The Little Mole' and 'The Little Spider' as well as a poetry book 'Love, Death and Madness'.

Printed in Great Britain
by Amazon

41347632R00136